Harry Lovegrove lives in Finchampstead, near Reading. *Rodney MacDoodle's Adventures Back in Time* is the first book he has written. He is a keen Leicester City fan and also works part time as a tennis coach. Harry is a Christian and is a member of Reading Family Church.

Harry Lovegrove

RODNEY MACDOODLE'S ADVENTURES BACK IN TIME

AUSTIN MACAULEY PUBLISHERS™

LONDON • CAMBRIDGE • NEW YORK • SHARJAH

A CIP catalogue record for this title is available from the British Library.

ISBN 9781035866717 (Paperback)
ISBN 9781035866724 (ePub e-book)

www.austinmacauley.com

First Published 2024
Austin Macauley Publishers Ltd®
1 Canada Square
Canary Wharf
London
E14 5AA

I would like to thank my parents for their loving support of me when writing this book. My mum did a fabulous job in helping to proofread and grammatically edit my book. My dad encouraged me not to doubt myself and send the book to a publisher. I would like to thank my grandma for all the encouragement she gave me when she read my manuscript.

I would also like to thank my friends who made some reviews and edits of the book. I really appreciated all the feedback.

Lastly, I would like to thank Austin Macauley Publishers for all their hard work in reviewing and publishing my book. I could not have published this without them.

Prologue

"Sandy, are you still here? You're supposed to be at the park for the football match. It's starting in five minutes."

A boy in his late teens, wearing the 1990 World Cup England football shirt, jumped up off his bed in horror. He had been lying down, listening to the radio on top of his bookcase, and had completely lost track of time. He wasn't even in his football kit.

Sandy rapidly opened his drawers and threw out the kit of his local football team, Inglefell, onto the bed. Once he had changed clothes, he rushed down the stairs to get his bike out of the garage.

He mounted his bike and bombed it down the roads, on one occasion pulling out in front of a car and narrowly avoiding being run over if it hadn't been for the driver slamming his foot on the brakes. The driver furiously hooted his horn and shook his fist at Sandy, who was gone in an instant.

Sandy reached the park in record time and dismounted from his bike. He rushed over to the rest of the Inglefell youth team, who were standing in a huddle.

"Coach, I'm so sorry I'm late," apologised Sandy. "I guess I just lost track of time."

"I'm not going to pretend I'm fine with this, Sandy," said the coach in an icy voice. "This isn't the first time you've been late. Stay behind at the end of the match. I would like to have a chat with you."

Sandy was in a grumpy mood as the match kicked off. Why had he let himself lose track of time? He had cycled recklessly just to be on time, almost getting himself killed in the process, and now he was in big trouble with the coach. His mood didn't improve when the other team's striker nutmegged him. He was the last defender, so he had to act fast.

He made a dangerous slide tackle but didn't win the ball. The boy he fouled was immediately on his feet and furiously grabbed hold of Sandy. Sandy looked into the other boy's eyes and noticed that they were strangely familiar. The boy also seemed to recognise Sandy and, instead of shoving him as he had planned, gave him a hug.

1

How It All Started

32 Years Later

"You guys will never guess what I've just found!" Rodney MacDoodle was in the attic with his brother and sister.

"What have you got there, Rod?" cried Dennis eagerly. At 11 years of age and being the youngest of the three, Dennis was the most energetic. He quickly dashed over to his older brother.

"Watch it, Dennis," warned Rod. "These floorboards up here aren't the safest."

"Sorry, I forgot," said Dennis. "But come on, what is it?" Rod passed an old, shabby cardboard box to Dennis and his older sister, Rosie, who, being 20, had followed at a more sedate pace.

They opened it up and the first thing they saw was a photograph of their parents, which had been taken many years ago.

"Gosh, Dad looks so young!" exclaimed Rosie. "And Mum, of course. I wonder when it was taken."

"It was before they were married, so over thirty years ago," said Rod. It was their parents' thirtieth wedding anniversary that day. "Look at Dad wearing his England World Cup t-shirt."

"He so desperately wanted to fit in with his friends," laughed Rosie.

Their dad, Sandy, was Scottish and had grown up in Aberdeen. His parents had moved to England, to the 'wee village Inglefell' as they liked to call it, in 1990, the year England got to the semi-final of the World Cup.

Being Scottish, Sandy at first had ridiculed the idea of supporting England at the World Cup that year, especially as Scotland had also qualified. But when Scotland didn't advance beyond the group stage, he decided he would support England for the rest of the tournament, seeing as it would make him popular with the friends he had just made at his new school. He even bought himself an England shirt, the one he was wearing in the photograph.

"Look, it's in here!" yelled Dennis and pulled that very same shirt out of the box. It was still in fairly good condition despite being stuffed away in a dusty box for many years. He tried it on, but it was far too big for him.

"Dad was seventeen when he bought it," laughed Rod. "It's far too big for you. Here, let me try it on."

Dennis passed the t-shirt to Rod, who tried it on and, despite him only being fourteen, it fit perfectly. Rod was fairly large for his age though and most people thought he was much older, like seventeen or eighteen.

Rod looked in the box again and saw an old newspaper. He reached down to pick it up, but it was so old that when he grabbed the first page, it ripped off.

"Be careful, Rod," said Rosie.

Rod carefully pulled the front cover into the light. The picture was of some drunk England supporters at the 1990 World Cup. They had evidently got themselves into trouble, like many other England fans.

He turned over the page and saw another article headlined 'Criminal Cop Captured'. He read that this policeman, Agustin De Baerdemaeker, who had completely misused his powers, was arrested in Inglefell and sentenced to fifteen years in prison.

Rod was just about to tell his siblings that their 'wee' village had got into a national newspaper when he was interrupted by a yell from downstairs.

"How are those chairs coming along?"

Rosie, Rod and Dennis glanced at each other sheepishly. They were supposed to be bringing down chairs for the big celebration dinner they were having in the evening for their parents' thirtieth wedding anniversary. Many family members and friends were coming, so they needed extra chairs which were stored up in the attic.

"We're bringing them down right now, Mum," called Rosie down the stairs.

"Well hurry up then," called Louise, their mum. "Also, can one of you quickly run down to the shop and buy some potatoes? We're running low and I need to put them in the oven soon. Dad has the car as he is picking up some of the guests from the station."

"Okay, I will," volunteered Rod. He had ripped out the article about the policeman and put it in his pocket, so that he could read it properly later.

"Thanks, Rod," said Louise, opening her purse. She pulled out a card and handed it to Rod. "Here, take this."

Rod, still wearing his dad's football shirt, was in deep thought as he walked to the corner shop. He recounted the story his parents would no doubt tell later that day of how they first met.

Sandy had been playing football for the Inglefell under-18s one day. He had made a couple of reckless tackles and a few of the boys on the opposite team were not impressed.

Three of the boys had beaten him up that night as he walked home, and he was found sometime later on the side of the road by Louise. She took him to her home and bandaged his wounds, while her parents were at the cinema. Louise, being a football fan herself, suggested they watch the rest of England's World Cup matches together.

The night of England's semi-final with Germany turned out to be an unforgettable night for both of them. Despite England's loss on penalties, they shared their first kiss that night. This started a relationship, which resulted in marriage two years later.

What a romantic story, thought Rod. *I wish I could have been there to see it. But I wasn't and I never will be because there's no such thing as time-travel—it only happens in stories or TV programmes.*

Rod suddenly remembered that the card-readers at the shop had broken and he didn't have any cash on him. However, he caught sight of a cash machine outside, so he walked up and entered his mum's pin—1990. Louise had first met Sandy in 1990, which made her pin number easy to remember.

When the card came back out, Rod was a little bit confused. Why had it not asked how much he wanted to withdraw? He re-inserted his card. Same result, the card was ejected after he entered the pin.

Rod turned around. "That doesn't wor…" He got the shock of his life. Everything looked different. The shops, the road, the cars in the small village carpark.

When Rod had walked up to the cash machine, he had passed a brand-new Tesla. He remembered thinking how amazing it looked and wished he could afford one of those when he bought his first car. It had now completely vanished.

Rod looked at all the cars that were parked outside the shop. Not one of them had a number plate in the new format, with the two numbers to show the year they were made. Instead, they were all in the old format, with the letter at the beginning. Every car in the car park was over thirty years old.

Rod was completely dumbfounded. There was no way that all the people here would be driving cars that old. Surely someone would have a newish car, even if not brand-new. Not only that, but the cars also looked quite new, yet they had old number plates. What was going on?

Rod noticed a receipt on the floor that someone must have accidentally dropped after taking out some cash. Rod quickly snatched it up. He read everything on it and gave a cry when he saw the date. It was 30 June 1990.

Rod couldn't believe it. He had gone back in time thirty-two years. And he had just been telling himself that time-travel only happened in stories!

2

The Imposter Policeman

Somebody walked past Rod and gave him a little shove into the cash machine. Rod turned in annoyance and recklessly lashed out. The guy who had shoved him fell to the ground and blood came out of his nose.

To Rod's horror, he saw the guy wearing a police uniform. He immediately regretted letting his temper get the better of him. The policeman wiped his nose, rose to his feet with a face like thunder and grabbed Rod by the scruff of the neck. He dragged him roughly to a secluded spot behind the shop, before seizing Louise's card out of Rod's hand.

"No," yelled Rod, as the policeman laughed at him. "Give that back!"

"I saw what 'appened there, young man; you suddenly appeared out of nowhere. Now do you mind telling me what's goin' on?"

"Why aren't you arresting me?" asked Rod cheekily, trying to show that he wasn't scared. The policeman's face went scarlet, but he stayed quiet for a few moments, evidently deep in thought.

"What I'm about to tell you, don't you dare repeat to no one; else, you won't never see this card again. Understand?" Rod nodded.

"Good," said the policeman. "I ain't no policeman. I don't 'ave no job. I'm 'omeless and barely 'ave enough money to eat. I used to be a policeman, but I lost my job, some stupid affair you don't want to 'ear about. I was ordered to 'and in my uniform but I refused. I've been on the run from the police ever since."

"Why didn't you hand in your uniform?" asked Rod.

"Cos I knew I would be 'omeless," replied the imposter policeman. "The police were gonna seize me 'ome as well. There was only one way I would be able to make money, that ain't begging. I would never let meself be classified as one of them people."

"How do you earn your money then?" asked Rod.

"I pretend to be a policeman. I watch out for people breaking the law and then I threaten to arrest them. Now, most people don't like being arrested—they'd do anything to get free. I just ask them 'ow much money they would give me. And that's 'ow I 'ave the money to eat."

"So why didn't you arrest me then and ask for a bribe?" said Rod.

"Because I saw you appear out of nowhere. You're not from this world, even though you're wearing that there football shirt. And you're gonna tell me your story, else you ain't getting this 'ere card back."

"Fine," said Rod. "I'm from the future, the year 2022. I was just withdrawing cash from the machine, when suddenly everything changed and I had gone back in time."

"Interesting," said the imposter. "You got money?"

"I'm not going to bribe you," said Rod. "You're not a policeman and you can't arrest me."

"But I do 'ave your card. And I reckon you need that to get back to your future. You give me five 'undred pounds next Friday and I give you your card back."

"What?" exclaimed Rod. "I don't have any money apart from these two notes! I won't be able to earn five hundred pounds in less than a week!"

"Not my problem," said the imposter. "You give me the money and you get your card back. Otherwise, you won't be able to get back to your world for a long time. And if or when you do, you will be much older. Everything will be completely different. Do you want that?"

"Of course not," said Rod. "But tell me, how am I supposed to earn that amount of money in a week?"

"I told you, it's not my problem. Just meet me in that spot over there, where we had our little discussion, next Friday and give me the money if you have it."

"Is that where you live?" asked Rod.

"That's none of your business!" yelled the imposter. "Now get on your way."

3

The Hero of Hunters Wood

Rod gladly fled from the imposter. He was in a right mess now—stuck in 1990 and the only way he could get back to 2022 was by giving that horrid man five hundred pounds in one week's time.

He had no clue where he could earn that sort of money. And even if he somehow managed to do so, would the imposter policeman keep his promise and give Rod his mum's card back?

Rod jogged to the local recreational ground. There were two football pitches, a cricket outfield, and some tennis courts. He saw there was a football match about to start, which surprised him as it was July, given the season normally ended in May.

Rod approached a middle-aged gentleman standing by the side of the pitch. "Who's playing?" he asked.

"It's the under-18s. We're playing a summer friendly match against Hunters Wood. You from around here?"

"I've lived here all my life," replied Rod.

"Hmm, I don't recognise you. Maybe I know your parents. What's your name?"

"Rodney MacDoodle."

"Oh, are you related at all to Maureen MacDoodle? Her family has recently moved here from Scotland. We work together."

Rod didn't know what to say. Maureen MacDoodle was his grandmother, but he couldn't say that. His grandmother was definitely not old enough to have grandchildren in 1990. This man would think he was a complete lunatic.

"Hey there, you, wearing the England shirt." Rod turned around, glad of the interruption. A man in his mid-thirties walked up to him. Rod guessed he was one of the managers. "How old are you?" the man asked.

"Why do you want to know?" asked Rod, feeling suspicious.

"One of our boys has come down with a sudden illness. I was wondering if you wanted to take his place today. But you need to be the right age to play."

"I'm fourteen."

"You're only fourteen," replied the manager, looking shocked. "Wow, you look a lot older. Don't worry, we'll just have to play with one less player then."

"Hey, wait a minute," cried Rod. "I can still play for you. Where I come from, I play in the under-18s, and I am every bit as good as the other players. Please let me play for you today. I won't let you down, I promise."

"Oh, alright," said the manager. "You can play then. It will be better than us being a player down. Come with me."

Rod followed the manager. As he was walking, he noticed a lad cycling into the park in football kit. The lad quickly jumped off his bike and ran over to join the other team, who were in a huddle.

"Looks like someone's late," Rod laughed to himself. "Oh, thank you."

The manager had picked up a t-shirt from a large bag and handed it to Rod. "Here, put that on and then I'll introduce you to the team. Hey, Tom. I've found us a replacement."

A tall, muscular lad ran over towards Rod and the manager.

"This is our captain, Tom," said the manager to Rod. "What's your name?"

"Rod MacDoodle."

"Nice to meet you, Rod," said the manager. "I'm Joe."

"Hey Rod," said Tom. "Come and meet the others."

Rod followed warily. Tom seemed nice enough, but he had seen a look on his face that said, *Don't mess with me.*

"What position am I playing?" asked Rod.

"Attacking midfield," replied Tom.

"Boys, are you ready?" yelled the referee.

"Oh bother, I don't have time to introduce you to the others now," said Tom, giving the ref a thumbs-up to show they were ready. "We'll have to do it at half-time."

The game started brightly with goals for both teams. One of the Inglefell boys scored a screamer which flew into the top left corner, giving the Hunters Wood goalkeeper no chance.

Then the ball was passed to Rod, and he was away. As Rod had told Joe, he did play for the Inglefell under-18s back home in 2022 (ironic as he was now playing against them), and he was a lot better than most of the older players in the team. He was too good for most of the 1990 Inglefell players and he worked his way through their defence.

Rod just had the last defender and goalie to beat. He skilfully nutmegged the defender and had a clear shot on goal.

He was about to shoot when the defender, who he had just nutmegged, turned around and slide-tackled Rod to the ground.

Both Rod and the defender rolled over each other. Rod grabbed hold of him and pulled back his arm to throw a punch. There was no chance he would have won the ball. It was a deliberate attempt to prevent him from scoring.

Rod looked straight into the defender's face. It was like he was looking in the mirror. That face was almost identical to his own.

Rod realised that the defender was his dad, Sandy. He quickly lowered his arm and instead gave Sandy a small hug.

"Rod, what do you think you're doing?" thundered Tom. "That was a professional foul. You would have scored if it wasn't for him."

"I know, it's just…" Rod quickly racked his brains to think of an excuse.

"Oh, forget it!" snapped Tom. "And for that, I'm taking this free kick, not you. So just get into the box and don't do anything else stupid."

Tom then turned to the referee. "Why did you only give him a yellow card?" he shouted. "That was a clear red!"

"How dare you speak to me like that?" said the referee in an icy voice, as he pulled out his yellow card and showed it to Tom. "Learn some respect or else you won't take part in the game."

Tom, with a hostile look on his face, stormed over to the ball and took the free kick. He blasted the ball straight at the wall with full power. The ball found a gap between players in the wall and went through to the goalkeeper, who fumbled it, due to the pace. The ball rolled over the line and Hunters Wood had equalised.

However, none of the Hunters Wood players were very happy. They didn't like Tom, their captain, and were disappointed with the disrespectful way he had spoken to Rod and the referee.

Even Tom was unhappy, despite the fact he had just scored. His frustration boiled over when Sandy, running past, accidentally trod on his foot. Tom lashed out and pushed Sandy to the ground. Sandy angrily rose to his feet and squared up to Tom. They both started shoving each other and the referee blew his whistle as he marched over towards them.

"Get off the field, both of you!" he roared, pulling his red card out of his pocket. "No, don't argue, just go! Disgraceful behaviour!"

"Look ref, it wasn't Sandy's fault," pleaded Rod. "Tom was the one that—"

"I said don't argue!" interrupted the ref. "My decision is final."

Five minutes later, it was half-time with the score being 1-1. The boys in both teams gloomily walked off to have their half-time team talks, due to the ugly scenes that had taken place. Everyone was glad to see Tom walking away in the distance.

"Look, boys," said Joe, to the Hunters Wood team. "I've just had a chat with Tom, and I told him to go home. I am disgusted at his behaviour. Dissent towards the referee is something I will not tolerate from any member of this team."

"Rod, I apologise for what Tom said to you, that was completely unacceptable. If you would rather not continue, I completely understand."

"No, I'll stay," replied Rod. "I'm going to help you win this match."

"Good lad," said Joe. "Thanks Rod, you're a real star. Right, boys, let's go out there and put in a match-winning performance. But whatever the outcome, I'm proud of you."

Rod smiled. What a nice man Joe was. He didn't know many football managers like that.

The Hunters Wood boys, inspired by Joe's half-time talk, had a much better second half. They created more chances and had more possession. However, the Inglefell defence was also brilliant and prevented most of the Hunters Wood shots from being on target.

Then the Inglefell striker broke away and fired a shot past the Hunters Wood goalkeeper and the ball clipped the inside of the post. It rolled along the goal line and hit the other post.

Fortunately for Hunters Wood, their goalie was quick to get back and pick up the ball before the Inglefell striker could tap the ball into the net. All the Hunters Wood players breathed a huge sigh of relief. That was too close.

Inglefell did manage to get the ball in the net a few minutes later. However, the linesman's flag went up as the striker was offside, so the goal didn't count.

"Come on boys, we've got ten minutes left," encouraged Joe. "Someone go and score that winning goal!"

Hunters Wood dominated the final ten minutes and put Inglefell under a lot of pressure. The Inglefell defence were feeling exhausted and knew they wouldn't be able to last much longer.

With half a minute left, Hunters Wood managed to get a shot on target. However, the Inglefell goalie produced a fantastic save, and the ball went out for a corner. This would be the last action of the match.

The corner was taken, and the ball came flying into the box. Rod saw the ball and flung himself at it. He managed to make contact with his head and direct the ball into the top left corner.

The Hunters Wood players dived on top of Rod. He had scored. They had won the match 2-1. Rod was the 'Hero of Hunters Wood'. He rose to his feet and shook hands with all the Inglefell players. They had played brilliantly, but just came up against a better team on the day.

Joe ran over and gave Rod a massive hug. "That was an outstanding performance there, Rod. I am so proud of you. You should also be extremely proud of yourself."

"I am," replied Rod, beaming. "Thank you so much."

"Can I talk to you alone for a moment?" asked Joe.

"Sure," said Rod and followed him to a quiet spot.

"Your football team is so lucky to have you, Rod," said Joe. "When you said that you were better than most of the under-18s, I have to admit I thought it was just bravado. But you're definitely the real deal, aren't you? Which club did you say you played for?"

"I didn't say," said Rod. "But you wouldn't know it. It's a long way from here. Don't worry, you won't be coming up against me anytime soon."

"I am glad to hear that," laughed Joe. "Look, I have a proposition for you. Earlier today, I told Tom that he is no longer welcome at this football club. Would you consider taking his place and joining the team? I know that you're only fourteen, but today you showed that you have a great deal of talent. You can go a long way in your career. Hunters Wood

Football Club will benefit hugely with having a player of your capabilities."

Rod knew full well he was trying to get back home to his own future world but didn't know how long it would take him to pay the imposter policeman. He wasn't quite sure what to do, or how to reply.

"I understand you need to think about it," said Joe understandingly. "Take as much time as you need. We usually train on Monday evenings. Our last training session is next Monday, so I hope that you will join us."

"Where do you train?" asked Rod.

"The big green in Hunters Wood, if you know where that is," replied Joe, looking at Rod, who nodded. "If you would like to join us, let me know and I will get in touch with your current club and see if we can transfer you in. Hunters Wood is a developing club you know. One day, we could be in the First Division. And you could be part of that."

It took Rod a moment to realise what Joe meant. He was talking about the Premier League. The Premier League had been known as the First Division up until 1992.

Wow, he thought to himself. *I could play in the Premier League. Maybe it wouldn't be so bad if I stayed here.*

"Well, it's been great meeting you today, Rod," said Joe, interrupting Rod's thoughts. "If you'll excuse me, I must go and speak to the others. But keep in mind my offer and let me know soon."

Rod walked back home, dreaming of being a future football star, maybe even playing with the likes of David Beckham. He could even play in the same team as him. How amazing would that be?

4

A Long-Awaited Conversation

It was seven o'clock on a Saturday evening in the tranquil Inglefell village. As it was summer, there were still about three hours of daylight left. The streets were quiet, no cars were driving on the roads. The only vehicle, if you can call it that, on the road was a bicycle, being ridden furiously by a boy in his late teens. That boy was called Sandy MacDoodle.

Sandy was in a bad mood. His team, Inglefell, had lost and he had unfairly been sent off. That big guy had just attacked him. Why had the ref sent him off as well? And to cap it all off, the Inglefell manager had made him stay behind another couple of hours to clean the changing room in the clubhouse. It just wasn't fair.

Sandy turned off the main road into the street behind his house. He recognised Rod as he passed him.

"That was really weird," Sandy said to himself. "Why did he hug me after I fouled him? And why does he look so familiar?"

Meanwhile, Rod was walking, in a world of his own, past his own house, the one he had lived his whole life in. He was eager to see what it looked like in 1990.

Rod caught sight of the house, minus the extension, which had been built when he was five. He had vaguely remembered how it previously looked, but seeing it now brought the image back to life.

Rod looked up and caught sight of Sandy, on his bike, watching him at the corner of the road. Sandy, aware that Rod was now looking at him, went red and cycled off. Rod followed him, knowing that his dad's first house in Inglefell was the one behind his own. As Rod turned into the street of his dad's house, he just caught a glimpse of Sandy turning into the driveway.

Rod quickened his pace and as he reached the driveway, saw his dad come out of the garage and walk in through the front door. He slipped into the garden and hid behind a bush. He desperately wanted to talk to his dad. To tell him about the predicament he now found himself in.

But he couldn't tell Sandy who he really was. Sandy likely wouldn't believe him, and besides, even if he did, that would just make things complicated. It would be dangerous telling his dad about his own future. It could cause him to do a few things differently to how he would have originally done them.

Rod was stumped. Who could he tell? Joe's face suddenly flashed into his mind.

"The Hunters Wood football manager?" he said to himself. "I'm sure I can trust him, and he certainly doesn't have anything to do with my future, at least not that I know of."

The front door suddenly opened, and Sandy walked out of the house and down the driveway, passing the bush that Rod was hiding behind but not seeing him. Rod slowly emerged from behind the bush when he saw Sandy disappear and silently walked out of the garden. He saw Sandy further along the pavement.

Rod also noticed a girl in her late teens walking along the other side of the road. What he didn't notice was that Sandy had stopped walking and was staring right at her. Rod was also staring at the girl because she looked somewhat familiar. However, unlike his dad, Rod carried on walking while looking at her and went straight into Sandy, almost knocking him over.

"Hey, watch it!" cried Sandy in annoyance.

"Sorry, Dad," apologised Rod.

"Why do you keep following me around?" asked Sandy frustratedly. "This is the third time we've met today." Sandy then realised what Rod had just said to him. "Did you just call me Dad?" he asked, puzzled.

Rod could have kicked himself. How could he have been so stupid. His face at once went as red as a beetroot.

"Did I? Sorry, I meant lad. Dad and lad, similar words."

"Hmmm. I don't think so. You have been behaving rather strangely today. I think you've got some explaining to do."

"Okay, but it's a long story."

"Well, it just happens that I'm going out on an evening walk. You've got plenty of time to tell your story, lad."

5

Like Father, Like Son

Rod desperately began to think about what he could tell his dad. He just didn't know what to say that would be believable. And he wasn't going to tell the truth.

Into his mind popped the story about his grandad's estranged brother. Sandy had only told Rod the previous night when they had been talking about some of the guests coming to the anniversary party. It seemed a lifetime ago to Rod, though not even twenty-four hours had passed for him.

Rod's grandad and great-uncle had been very close when growing up but fell out in their early twenties. When Rod's great-uncle moved from Aberdeen to Bristol, he never kept in touch with his brother.

While growing up, Sandy had never known about his uncle. Then one day when he was seventeen, for some reason, he was talking with his dad, Angus, and asked him if he had any siblings.

Angus went quiet for a few moments. Then his wife, Maureen, who was also there, nudged him. "Come on, Angus, you've got to tell him. He's seventeen, he needs to know."

Once Angus had slowly murmured the story to him, Sandy made up his mind. He was going to Bristol the following weekend to meet his estranged family.

The first person Sandy met was his cousin, Robert. They became best friends and grew so close that their dads eventually resolved the argument, albeit after much persuading from their wives.

Rod thought about pretending to be one of Robert's brothers. He just didn't know if he could go along with it. Could he really lie to his dad like that? But what was the alternative? To tell him the truth?

"Why is life so hard?" Rod asked himself, under his breath.

Rod made up his mind. He was going to make up a brother for Robert, called Rodney, and pretend to be him. "You may find this hard to believe, Sandy, but you're my cousin."

"But I don't have any cousins," said Sandy in surprise. "Just a younger brother. Neither of my parents have siblings."

"Then your dad has lied to you," replied Rod. "Because my dad is his brother. They fell out when they were in their early twenties. My dad used to live in Scotland, but he moved down to Bristol many years ago."

"What? How? This doesn't make sense. My dad doesn't have any brothers." said Sandy, looking completely shocked.

"He does," replied Rod. "Your dad is my uncle. Has he really not told you about us?"

"No, he hasn't," said Sandy curtly, with an angry look on his face. "So how did you know we live here? We only recently moved from Scotland."

"Your mum has always been in touch with mine. They were close friends before the argument, and I think they both want their husbands to resolve things. My mum is very keen for our families to make up. That's why she suggested I come here for a few days and meet you."

"Wow, I can't believe my parents would keep this from me," said Sandy in disgust. "Wait till I get home and give them a piece of my mind."

Rod inwardly groaned. He certainly hadn't meant to cause a rift between Sandy and his parents. And if Sandy mentioned him? Rod didn't dare think about what might happen. He had to do something to stop Sandy telling them.

Rod then remembered how stubborn his grandad could be. After all, his dad had told him that it had taken a great deal of persuasion from him and his mum to get Angus to forgive his brother and make up.

"No, that's not a good idea, not if you want them to sort out their differences so that we can be reunited as a family," Rod said to Sandy quietly. "Uncle Angus is stubborn; you should know that better than me. If you make him feel guilty about the whole affair, it will only make him more stubborn."

"What should I do then?" asked Sandy. "If I don't say anything, our families will never reunite."

"But if you accuse him and make him feel guilty, we certainly won't be reunited," replied Rod. "First you need to take a few days to cool down before you say anything. Once you've cooled down, maybe innocently ask your dad if he has any siblings. And then if he does open up, you can gently suggest to him that they patch up their differences."

"Fine," said Sandy with a huff. "But it's not right that they've kept this from me."

"No, it certainly isn't," said Rod, who was feeling very guilty about lying to Sandy. He had to keep telling himself that it was a good thing what he was doing. That his words to Sandy would bring about a happy reunion.

But what would happen then? Sandy would meet his cousins and find out that they'd never heard of Rod. Sandy would know that Rod had been lying to him. Rod's face burned at the thought of it. Rod didn't want to have to tell Sandy any more lies so he decided to change the topic of conversation. But what could he talk about?

He looked down at his England t-shirt. Of course, it was the summer of 1990. The football world cup would be happening now, wouldn't it? His dad was a massive football fan.

"Been following the football?" asked Rod casually.

"Of course," said Sandy, who was now starting to cheer up after the shock of finding out about his estranged cousins. "We're playing Cameroon in the quarters tomorrow night. Can you believe it, England are actually in the World Cup quarterfinals."

"I know, right," laughed Rod. "It's unusual to see us coming this far in a major tournament."

"Yes, it is pretty unusual, especially as we haven't been at our best recently," replied Sandy, his eyes now lighting up. "But what a match that was last week against Belgium, though. Did you see that volley from David Platt? Just one minute left on the clock and he came up with that. I was certain we would have our first ever World Cup penalty shootout."

Rod knew that England would go on to lose on penalties to Germany (West Germany back then) in the semis, but he didn't say anything. That was really all he knew about the

1990 World Cup—England's defeat to West Germany in the semi-finals.

Everything suddenly came back to Rod. His parents shared their first kiss on the night of the semi-final. Had they met? He remembered that girl he had seen earlier, the one who looked strangely familiar. It had been his mum.

And why had he bumped into Sandy? It wasn't just because he hadn't been looking where he was going. No, Sandy must have also been looking at her.

Rod knew that Sandy had suddenly switched to supporting England halfway through the World Cup. He had said it because it would make him popular with his friends, but what if it was one friend in particular? What if it was Louise? Rod decided to bite the bullet.

"May I ask you why you're supporting England?" he asked. "I mean, you are Scottish, aren't you?"

"Yes, but I do live in England now," replied Sandy. "And since Scotland got knocked out, what reason do I have not to?"

"Because you're Scottish. Scottish people don't suddenly start supporting England for no reason. Come on Sandy, we're family, you can tell me why."

"Okay, I will. But you must promise not to tell anyone."

"My lips are sealed," said Rod, eager to hear his dad's secret.

"Well, there's this girl at school, Louise Johnson. She is a dedicated England fan. If she knows that I'm also supporting England, then she will like me better."

Rod smiled. Louise Johnson was his mum's maiden name. His dad had fallen in love with his mum. And for that reason, he had started supporting England. It was so romantic.

6

A Fight and an
Unexpected Meeting

It was starting to get dark, so they decided to turn around and head home.

"I don't suppose you have anywhere to stay for the night?" asked Sandy.

Rod could have kicked himself. With all that had gone on today, he hadn't even thought about where he would sleep.

"No, I don't," he replied, looking flustered. "What am I going to do?"

"Don't worry," Sandy reassured him. "We have a guest bedroom. You can stay with us for a couple of nights. Maybe when Dad sees you, he'll want to try and make things up with his brother."

"No, I can't do that," cried Rod in horror, knowing full well that his lies would be exposed. "Your dad doesn't want anything to do with my family. He has made that perfectly clear. You're the one who needs to speak to your dad about this, not me."

"Okay," said Sandy. "Guest bedroom not an option then. We have a shed in the bottom of the garden, though. I can bring you down a camp bed and put you up there for a couple of nights."

"That would be so kind of you," replied Rod gratefully, now feeling extremely guilty that Sandy was repaying his lies with such kindness.

"That's what family is for," said Sandy warmly, as he gave Rod a hug. "Hello, what do we have here?"

A large person was standing in front of them blocking their way.

"I've been looking for you!" he said in a loud voice. Rod recognised that voice and trembled; it was Tom.

"I have a bone to pick with both of you," he said threateningly. "Nobody tackles me dirty and gets away with it."

"Look, we both know that's not true," said Sandy in a brave voice. "I accidentally trod on your foot, and you hurled me to the ground."

Rod looked at Sandy admiringly; he was dealing with this situation in a calm and responsible way.

Tom then turned on Rod. "As for you, little coward, Rodney, I believe you got me kicked out of the team."

"I think that was mostly your own doing," said Rod who had now plucked up a lot of courage, after watching how Sandy had dealt with him. "You seem to be an expert at screwing up your own life."

Rod immediately regretted saying that and opened his mouth to apologise. However, Tom, whose face had gone purple, spoke first.

"How dare you speak to me like that, you little brat!" he thundered. "Do you want to take me on in a fight?"

"There's two of us and one of you," replied Rod coolly, his good intentions now vanished.

"Oh, that's what you think," sneered Tom.

Rod suddenly found his arms being seized from behind him. He looked across and saw that exactly the same thing had happened to Sandy.

"Nobody messes with me and gets away with it!" Tom yelled aggressively. "Now who wants to take the first punch?"

Rod painfully opened his eyes. His face was in agony. He saw his dad lying unconscious on the ground next to him. He gingerly rolled over to face him.

"Sandy, wake up," he hoarsely whispered.

Sandy didn't respond. Rod lifted up his arm and shook Sandy by the shoulder.

"Wake up!" he said, this time in a much louder voice.

Sandy opened his eyes and looked dazedly at Rod.

"Where are we?" he asked quietly. "And how did we get here?"

"We were on a walk," Rod answered him. "And then we met that horrid Tom. The guy who was playing football with us earlier. Don't you remember?"

"Oh yes," said Sandy, who was gradually regaining consciousness. "It's all coming back to me. The question is, can we get home? We've still got quite a way to go."

"I don't think I'll be up to it," replied Rod forlornly, as he gazed into the distance.

He caught sight of a young lady jogging on the footpath in their direction.

"Over here!" he yelled, waving frantically at her.

The lady saw Rod waving and came over. As she came into view, Rod realised she was still in her teens.

"What happened to you guys?" she asked. "Is that you, Sandy MacDoodle?"

"Ay, it's me all right," said Sandy. "We both got into a fight and came off worse."

"I can see that," she replied and then turned to Rod. "I don't think we've met before. I'm Louise Johnson and you are…"

"Rodney MacDoodle," he answered.

"Another MacDoodle," replied Louise, smiling. "You two must be related then?"

"We're cousins," said Rod. "Please can you help us get home?"

"I'll go one better and take you to my house. You're both covered in bruises, and I need to treat them fairly quickly."

Louise then suddenly grabbed hold of Rod and pulled him to his feet. A moment later, Sandy also found himself on his feet.

"This isn't going to be easy," said Louise. "We're half a mile away from home."

However, Louise was extremely strong and managed to support both Rod and Sandy all the way.

It suddenly occurred to Rod as they were walking that this was his own mother helping them. She had said her name was Louise Johnson, but it hadn't clicked in the shock of the moment.

The story of how his parents met immediately came back to Rod, that his dad had been beaten up and was found at the side of the road by his mum. And now he was experiencing it first-hand.

"My parents are out tonight at the cinema," said Louise as they walked up to the front door. "They said they'd be back at about one, which is good as that's still two hours away and I don't particularly want them to find me with two young men in the house."

As soon as they were inside, Louise made them both lie down on sofas.

"I'll go and get you both something to put on those bruises," said Louise and quickly popped out of the room.

"Is Louise the girl you were telling me about earlier?" Rod asked Sandy in a low voice.

"Yes she is but be quiet about it," hissed Sandy.

"The reason you're supporting England in the World Cup," said Rod cheekily, watching Sandy go red.

Sandy was just about to retort when Louise came back in. Louise was a massive football fan herself and was very pleased to hear the subject being brought up.

"Did I hear you guys talking about the football?" she asked them.

"Yes, we were," replied Rod. "Sandy can't wait for the quarterfinal."

"Well, he won't have to wait long," said Louise. "It's tomorrow night against Cameroon. Though I must say, it's very interesting, Sandy, that you're excited for an England football match. Particularly as you were such a devoted Scotland fan at the start of the World Cup. I also recall you saying the time you knew you had gone mad was the time you supported England."

"I said no such thing," cried Sandy in denial. "And anyway, after Scotland got knocked out in the group stages, what possible reason would I have for not supporting England, especially as everyone else in the class is? Don't want to be the odd one out, do I?"

"I was only teasing," said Louise, with a twinkle in her eye. "Besides, I've seen you walking down the street plenty of times with your England football t-shirt on; the one Rod is wearing at the moment."

"Oh no, this is mine," said Rod.

"Yes, it's his," said Sandy. "Mine's in my bedroom, waiting for me to wear tomorrow for the big match."

"Are you having anyone around tomorrow to watch it?" asked Louise.

"No, why?" replied Sandy in surprise.

"Well, I was wondering if the two of you would like to come here to watch it with me."

"Yes, we would love to," answered Rod and Sandy simultaneously.

7

The Beautiful Game of Football

At half seven the next evening, Rod and Sandy both turned up at Louise's house to watch the World Cup Quarter Final. Louise let them both in and invited them to make themselves comfortable on the sofa.

As Rod sat down, he felt something hard pressing against his leg from inside his trouser pocket. He pulled out the object and found it was his smartphone. He had had absolutely no idea he had been carrying it with him this whole time.

He immediately tried to switch it on. Nothing happened. The screen stayed blank. After pressing the power button several times, Rod knew it wouldn't work. It must have malfunctioned as a result of the time-travel.

Rod also felt a sheet of paper in his pocket. He pulled it out. The paper was blank, and its sides were rough. It had obviously been torn. *Strange,* thought Rod. *Why would he have torn a piece of paper and put it in his pocket?*

Rod suddenly remembered the newspaper in the attic. He had been reading an article about Inglefell, his hometown. He had felt so thrilled when reading about his hometown in a national newspaper.

Rod didn't fully read the article, so he had torn it out of the paper and put it in his pocket for him to read later. But with all that had happened to him over the past couple of days, Rod had completely forgotten about it. It had been about that crook, whatever his name was, who had been arrested in Inglefell.

Rod found it strange that the paper should now be blank. Nothing was written on it at all. Rod soon guessed why though; the newspaper had been published on 7 July 1990. He had seen the date on the front cover. However, it was only 1st July, so the events recorded hadn't happened yet, hence the newspaper sheet was blank.

Rod then groaned as he realised the enormity of the situation. As these events on the paper had not yet occurred, they could easily be altered. The whole course of history could be altered due to his time-travel—and he would be responsible.

Louise heard Rod's groan as she switched on the television.

"Are you alright?" she asked him, looking concerned.

"I'm fine," said Rod. "Don't worry about me."

"What have you got there?" asked Louise, as she saw Rod holding his phone and the newspaper article.

"Nothing," replied Rod, quickly putting them back in his pocket.

Louise was puzzled by Rod's behaviour, and she would have asked him some more questions if it hadn't been for Sandy letting out a yell as the highlights of England's previous match were being shown.

"What a goal! Did you guys see that? The last minute of extra time. Incredible."

This change of subject caused Louise to drop the issue, though she still felt Rod was hiding something. Whatever was that object he had been holding? She had never seen anything like it before.

As Rod started watching the build up to the match, he became nervous when it showed Cameroon's route to the quarters. They had beaten Argentina in their very first match and finished top of their group. They gone on to defeat Columbia in the last-16, so were looking quite strong.

England, on the other hand, had struggled through their group stage, with draws against the Republic of Ireland and Netherlands, before beating Egypt in their final match to top the group on four points. They had then needed one hundred and nineteen minutes to break the deadlock in their last-16 match against Belgium. Cameroon had definitely been the better team so far in the tournament.

Rod recognised a few of the England players as they walked out onto the pitch for the national anthems—people like Stuart Pearce, Gary Lineker and Paul Gascoigne. During the anthems, he didn't feel the usual tingle running down his spine like normal; he knew the result, England would win and reach the semis.

Cameroon started the match brightly, but in the twenty-fifth minute, against the run of play, England opened the scoring. A beautiful cross by Stuart Peace was headed home by David Platt, who was standing on the edge of the six-yard box. Both Sandy and Louise celebrated wildly and hugged each other. Rod watched them in delight.

Cameroon came back at them, creating several chances, but couldn't find the equalising goal before half-time.

Louise went to the kitchen at half-time and brought back some popcorn. "Think we'll win?" she asked Rod, offering him some of the popcorn.

"'Course we will," replied Rod. "It's coming home."

"What's coming home?" said Louise, looking confused. "What are you talking about?"

Rod could have kicked himself. That song, *Three Lions*, wasn't released until 1996 for the Euros.

"Never mind," he said. "You'll understand in a few years."

Both Sandy and Louise exchanged confused glances and Rod went red. Fortunately for him, the players were starting to come out for the second half, and nothing more was said.

Pearce and Platt linked up again at the start of the second half, this time the ball being crossed along the ground, but blocked by the Cameroon goalkeeper N'Kono.

"I hope they won't regret that," said Sandy.

"They won't," Rod muttered under his breath.

Cameroon then created a chance with the ball being played through to Roger Milla, their star player that tournament, and he was brought down in the penalty box by Paul Gascoigne. To the horror of the three watching, the referee pointed to the penalty spot. That wasn't in the script, was it?

Emmanuel Kunde stepped up and blasted the penalty into the top right corner, just escaping the hands of the diving Peter Shilton, the England goalkeeper.

Rod was completely dumbfounded when, five minutes later, Milla played through Eugene Ekeke, and he scored to give Cameroon the lead. What was going on? England had won this match, hadn't they? They reached the semis this year.

A horrible thought came to Rod. What if something was messing with the course of history, changing the outcome of this football match? He had watched *Back to the Future* many times. What if the same thing was happening, only this time in real life?

Rod suddenly went cold as he thought of the plot of Back to the Future; how Marty McFly had prevented his parents first meeting each other. This almost caused him to be completely erased from time. And Rod began to realise that he too was hindering his parents' relationship.

He knew that they shared their first kiss after England's loss to Germany in the semi-finals. Would him being there prevent that? Wouldn't they feel uncomfortable kissing each other with him in the room? Rod knew he needed to let them spend more time on their own.

Time was ticking on. The match had passed the 80-minute mark and England were still 2-1 down. Rod was convinced something else other than him was messing with time and changing history. Someone else may be preventing England from reaching the semis of the World Cup. Rod just wished life could go back to how it was, that he could return to 2022 and leave this complicated world behind.

Both England and Cameroon were still creating chances though, so Rod didn't completely give up hope. Gascoigne had played through David Platt, but his shot was just wide of the right post. Then Francois Omam-Biyik was played through, and he tried a cheeky backheel, but the shot was stopped by Peter Shilton.

Then, in the eighty-second minute, Gary Lineker was fouled in the penalty box. To the relief of the three watching, the ref blew his whistle and pointed to the penalty spot. Sandy and Louise both cheered loudly. Rod puffed out his cheeks.

"Come on, Gary, you've got this," said Rod, as Lineker stepped up to take the penalty. He calmly placed the ball on the penalty spot and walked back to the edge of the box. He ran up and smashed the ball into the right of the goal, as Cameroon's keeper N'Kono dived the wrong way.

Sandy and Louise celebrated wildly again, and this time Rod joined them. England were back in this. It was 2-2 with seven minutes to go. Could they find a late winner, or was it going to extra time?

The answer was extra time. The ref blew the full-time whistle and England were going the distance.

"That's two matches in a row now for England that have gone to extra time," informed Sandy. "First Belgium, now Cameroon."

"Hopefully, if we go on to win this, our players won't be too tired for the semi with West Germany," said Louise.

Extra time started and Rod, Louise and Sandy all watched the television nervously, though Rod was a bit more confident than the other two. England would surely go on and win this now.

Gary Lineker was played through on goal right at the end of the fifteen-minute first half. He was one-on-one with the goalkeeper but one of the defenders caught him up quickly.

Lineker played the ball to the left of the goalie, who had come rushing off his line to the edge of the penalty box to meet him. Both the goalie and the defender made contact with him, and he went down. The ref awarded England another penalty. This was the third of the match.

This time Lineker went the other way, towards the left of the goal. Again, the goalie went the wrong way and England were in the lead. Rod, Louise and Sandy all yelled at the tops of their voices, jumped up and down and hugged each other madly.

Rod suddenly realised his level of excitement matched that of the time when he had watched England in the 2018 World Cup and Euro 2021. This was a magical experience for him.

England really should have sealed the match in the second half of extra time. First Lineker had a great chance to get his hat-trick, but his shot went agonisingly wide of the left post. Then Trevor Steven crossed the ball into the box, but the ball somehow eluded Linker and Platt.

However, these missed chances didn't cost England. The ref finally blew the full-time whistle on extra time and England had won. They had defeated Cameroon 3-2 and were in the semi-finals of the World Cup for the first time since 1966, the year they won.

Most importantly, though for Rod, nothing had changed history. England were in the semi-finals of the 1990 World Cup.

8

A Risky Plan

The next evening, Rod walked over to Hunters Wood to attend their football team's training session, as it was Monday. He decided he would tell Joe, the Hunters Wood manager, about his situation at the end of the session.

Rod needed help to get back to his future pretty soon. After all, he couldn't sleep in the rotting, disused shed at the bottom of Sandy's garden forever. Sooner or later he would be found by Sandy's parents and then he would be in hot water.

Also, it wasn't fair on Sandy to keep asking him to sneak food out to him from the kitchen each day. Sandy had been very kind to him, letting him stay and keeping it a secret from his parents, who must surely now be wondering why all their food is disappearing so quickly.

A pang of conscience smote Rod as he realised how badly he was treating Sandy; lying about who he was and taking advantage of him in this manner. He just didn't know how he could resolve this though. There was absolutely no way he could tell him the truth.

The opportunity for Rod to speak to Joe arose when Joe approached him to ask whether he would like to join the team for the next season.

"Unfortunately, I don't think I will be able to," said Rod when Joe asked him. "It's quite complicated, can I talk to you about it?"

"Go ahead," replied Joe, feeling a little disappointed at missing the chance to coach such a talented footballer. "I'm all ears."

"Well," Rod began, "you probably won't believe me, but I promise, everything I'm about to tell you is the truth. I wish it wasn't, but unfortunately it is."

"I'm not from this world. I mean, I am from Earth—I'm not an alien. But I'm not from this time period. I have come from the future, the year 2022."

Joe looked astonished. Then he smiled. "Haha, that's a good one. You almost had me fooled then."

"No, I'm being serious. You remember one of the Inglefell boys—the guy who fouled me and got sent off? He's my dad."

Joe raised an eyebrow, not believing him at all. "Look kid, if you've just come here to waste my time—"

"No sir, I honestly haven't. Look, do you remember when the guy fouled me, and I grabbed him and was about to shove him?"

"Yes, you hugged him instead. I was confused about that."

"I hugged him because I recognised him. I knew he was my dad. You must believe me now."

"I kind of believe you, but I still have one question. Why are you telling me all this?"

"Because I need your help. Look, when I went back in time, it was through a cash machine. I literally just put in my card and entered my pin. And suddenly, I was here. I had gone back in time.

"Then a guy dressed in a policeman uniform, who isn't actually a policeman, stole my card and won't give it back unless I give him five hundred pounds by the weekend."

"I know the guy, the one pretending to be a policeman," said Joe surprisingly. "My brother is a policeman, the superintendent of this district actually. That policeman you met—his name is Agustin De Baerdemaeker. He is currently on trial for abusing his powers as a policeman. I won't go into full detail. But basically, he's a crook. You don't need to mess with him.

"When Agustin found out that he was being put on trial, he disappeared. The police have been looking for him ever since. There have been many reports of a policeman bribing people so they can avoid arrest, but so far, the police have been unsuccessful. Tell me all you know about him."

"Well, he told me his story," said Rod, feeling very relieved that Joe now believed him and would hopefully be able to help him get back. "But it was quite different from what you said so he's obviously twisted things. He's ordered me to give him five hundred pounds, which I don't have, at the weekend."

"He's meeting you somewhere?" asked Joe, his eyes lighting up.

"Behind one of the corner shops in Inglefell on Friday."

Joe whistled in delight. "Oh, that is brilliant, absolutely fantastic. My brother is going to be as pleased as punch. The police have been searching for Agustin for ages. And now they can find him, thanks to you."

"I'm going to have to meet with him though," said Rod.

"Certainly not, you should be nowhere near him. Things could get ugly, you know."

"But he has my card. I need it to get back to my future."

"Look, I will get it back for you."

"You don't know what the card looks like. I do. I need to do this."

Joe went quiet for a few minutes. Then his face lit up. "I've got a plan. It will be risky, but it means you won't be around when the police get there, as things are likely to get nasty then. Now, if we turn up before the police come, I will get Agustin away and have a chat with him; he doesn't know me. While I'm talking with Agustin, you search through his bag or coat or whatever and find that card.

"When you find the card, go straight to the cash machine and get back to your world. Agustin will go back and wait for you. However, instead of meeting you, he's going to find a whole load of policemen waiting to take him straight to jail, where he belongs. Now, whatever you do, do not tell anyone about this. It must be kept confidential. Do you understand?"

"Yes sir," said Rod. "See you on Friday then."

"Good. Now, under no circumstances must you meet Agustin again. If he gets away, you have no idea what trouble he could cause."

9

An Evening of Heartache and Joy

Rod spent most of the next few days on his own. It was only the beginning of July, so Sandy's college hadn't yet broken up for the summer. He, of course, was seventeen, so in his final year of A-levels.

The only real excitement for Rod came on Wednesday evening. It was the semi-final of the World Cup. England were playing West Germany. Like with the quarterfinal against Cameroon, Rod and Sandy both watched the match at Louise's house.

This time, Rod was not looking forward to the match. He knew exactly what was going to happen; he'd seen the highlights many times.

The first half wasn't very eventful. Not many chances were created, and it was goalless when both teams headed off the pitch at half-time.

Things started to get interesting though midway through the second half. In the sixtieth minute, West Germany opened the scoring.

One of the England defenders, Stuart Pearce, had committed a foul on the edge of the penalty area, so West Germany had a good chance of scoring.

The Germans, instead of playing the ball into the penalty area, tried to catch England out by passing short to Andreas Brehme. Brehme took a shot at goal, which was charged down by the England full-back, Paul Parker.

However, as the ball hit Parker, it looped in the air, straight over the goalkeeper Peter Shilton, and into the goal, giving West Germany a 1-0 lead.

After the goal, England went on the attack. They threw everything but the kitchen sink at the Germans. The German defence held together until the eightieth minute.

An England ball was played into the penalty area, which the German defence failed to clear. The ball went to Gary Lineker, who fired a powerful shot into the bottom right hand corner of the goal. England had equalised and the score was 1-1 with ten minutes of play left.

The final ten minutes came and went. The ref blew for full-time, and England were going to have to play another thirty minutes. It was the third match in a row where England had been taken to extra time.

The thirty minutes of extra time were pretty lively; there were several chances, but neither team managed to score. The closest chance was a shot from Chris Waddle, which hit the post.

Paul Gascoigne also made headlines, but for the wrong reasons. He went in for a reckless slide tackle—one he immediately regretted. He had already been booked a couple of times that tournament, so when the referee pulled the yellow card out of his pocket, he knew that he would be missing the World Cup final if England progressed.

Tears came into his eyes and Rod felt extremely sorry for him. It was a footballer's dream to play in the World Cup final. And he had messed it up because of one moment of thoughtlessness.

At this point, Rod noticed that Sandy and Louise, who were sat next to each other, were holding hands. The story of how they got together came back to him. They shared their first kiss that night. Rod knew that they would never kiss while he was there. He murmured something about going to the toilet and walked out of the room.

However, he stayed by the door and watched them, knowing they couldn't see him and didn't know he was there. He was also able to see the television from where he was standing, so he could still watch the football.

To Rod's complete and utter astonishment, England scored again. A free kick was whipped into the box and David Platt headed the ball into the net. Rod once again had that horrible feeling that something else had got back in time and was messing with the football matches.

Sandy and Louise both jumped up and kissed each other. But their celebration was short-lived. The referee held his hand up to indicate that David Platt was offside. The goal was not going to count.

Having seen Sandy and Louise kiss, Rod knew it was safe to come back in for the final few minutes of extra time. Again, both sides had chances—West Germany hit the post—but neither side scored, and the match was going to penalties.

Gary Lineker stepped up to take England's first penalty and drilled it into the bottom left corner to put them 1-0 up in the shootout.

Andreas Brehme went first for Germany and also drilled it into the bottom left. Peter Shilton went the right way but couldn't get a hand to it. 1-1.

Peter Beardsley was next up for England. It was a powerful shot into the top right corner. 2-1 England.

Lothar Matthaus, the German captain, blasted the ball into the left hand side to make it 2-2.

David Platt took England's third penalty. The German keeper Bodo Illgner guessed the right way and managed to get a hand to the shot. But David Platt had struck the ball firmly and it managed to find its way into the goal. 3-2.

Karl-Heinz Riedel took the sixth penalty of the shootout. It was a powerful penalty into the top left corner to make it 3-3.

Then it was Stuart Pearce's turn. Unfortunately, his penalty went straight down the middle and was saved by Illgner. West Germany had the advantage in the shootout.

Olaf Thon put his penalty in the right corner to give the Germans full advantage at 4-3.

Chris Waddle stepped up, knowing he had to score if England were to stay in the World Cup. His shot was powerful, too powerful. The ball was blasted straight over the crossbar and England were out. West Germany were through to face Argentina in the final.

Despite England's loss, Rod felt a strange sense of happiness. The right result had happened in the football match—nothing had been changed. Sandy and Louise were together. All was well at the moment—now he just needed to get back to his future, which of course was easier said than done. But he was too happy to think about it at that moment.

He looked across at Sandy and Louise, who were both smiling but trying to hide their smiles. After all, England had lost. But they had kissed each other, and they realised they were both in love with each other. This made them realise that there is much more to life than football.

10

A Dramatic Evening

Rod woke with an uneasy feeling. He at first wondered why, and then he realised. Today was the day. He was hopefully going to go back to his future—if all went to plan.

Rod spent the next few hours worrying over what would happen, what he would need to do. He headed over to the shops at half six that evening, where he would meet Joe. He breathed a sigh of relief when he saw Joe waiting there for him. Joe was a responsible adult and he felt safe with him.

Joe went through the plan again with Rod just so they were both clear.

"I have the money on me," said Joe. "Just in case. The most important thing here is that you get back to your world. Me and my brother will take care of the rest. Now, where did Agustin agree to meet you?"

"Over there, behind that shop," said Rod, pointing at the corner shop.

Joe walked to the store, crept around the ide, and came back to Rod a few moments later. "He's there," said Joe in a hushed whisper. "You know what you have to do."

Rod nodded and followed Joe to the store.

"Stay here," whispered Joe as he walked around the back of the store. Joe was dressed in a filthy outfit, which stank horribly. He approached Agustin. "Excuthe me," he lisped. "Can you spare any change for a poor old beggar like me?"

"Go away," snarled Agustin. "And mind your own business."

Joe was not going to be put off that easily. "Watcha doin' there?" he asked.

"I told you to mind your own business. I got better things to do than stand 'ere chattin' with a dirty, smelly beggar like you."

Joe saw Agustin's jacket on the ground nearby. Quick as lightning, Joe had grabbed the bag and was away, hoping Agustin would chase after him.

"Oi you, COME BACK 'ERE!" thundered Agustin, and leaped to his feet. He sprinted after Joe, leaving his big rucksack on the ground.

As soon as Agustin had gone, Rod was in there.

"Find the card and go to the cash machine," he told himself. He searched through the rucksack, but it was fairly large, so it was going to take him a good few minutes to find the card.

Joe, meanwhile, hadn't strayed too far as he was afraid that Agustin would go back and find Rod. Agustin, however, was dead keen on finding Joe.

You see, Rod's card was not in Agustin's rucksack as Joe and Rod thought, but in his jacket, which Joe was currently holding. Agustin needed to get his jacket back because he wanted Rod to get back to his own future. Secretly, he was afraid of Rod. Rod seemed too clever for his own good.

Agustin was worried that if Rod didn't disappear to his own world very soon, he may spoil all his plans.

Joe had been hiding behind the village petrol station for a few minutes now, watching Agustin, who was searching high and low, going into each store: the chemist, the post office, the newsagents, and not having much luck. Things would have been okay if it hadn't been for the owner of the petrol station, who spotted Joe hiding.

"Oi, what are you doing crouching here on my property? Clear off at once, else I'll call the police."

Joe sheepishly stood up and at that exact moment, Agustin came out of the newsagents.

"AY!" he yelled and sprinted towards Joe.

Joe turned and ran, but Agustin was fast, extremely fast. He had caught up with Joe in no time. He grabbed hold of Joe's shoulder. Joe turned around to see Agustin's large fist heading towards his face. He tried to dodge but wasn't fast enough.

Joe, feeling the full force of a large man's punch, fell to the ground with a bleeding nose. Agustin walked up to him and picked up his jacket.

"This is mine, I do believe," he said, and turned around to walk back to his place behind the store.

Rod had been having absolutely no luck whatsoever. He had searched through the rucksack twice. Three times. Still nothing. Then he heard a shout.

"Hey, why are you snooping through my dad's stuff?"

Rod turned around and his heart sank. It was Tom, the bully who had beaten up him and Sandy.

"You?" sneered Tom. "Couldn't stay away, I see. Well, my dad isn't going to have any of this. I'm taking you straight to him."

Tom roughly grabbed Rod and marched him out from behind the store. They bumped straight into Agustin.

"Ah, so you're 'ere," said Agustin, in a pleased tone. "Does this mean you've got the money?"

"Dad, I caught him snooping through your rucksack," said Tom.

"Snoopin' you say," replied Agustin. "You weren't by any chance lookin' for this, were you?"

Agustin pulled the card out of his coat pocket and showed it to an astonished Rod.

"Trying to get this back without paying, were you? Well, this won't do at all. You now owe me double."

"Now wait a minute," said Rod. "We had a…"

"Don't worry, sir, he gave me the money for safe keeping."

Joe's face appeared from behind Agustin and in his hand was five hundred pounds.

"Ah, so you two were working together I see. Well unluckily for yer, yer plan failed. And yer now owe me double."

"Look, I'll give you the full one thousand pounds. Just promise to give the card back to Rod first."

"Oh, I most certainly will, I'll be glad to get rid of the young scoundrel. Proper nuisance 'e is."

Joe gave Agustin the money once he had given Rod his card. "Go on, get outta 'ere quick, before I change me mind."

Rod took the card and fled, with Joe close behind him. They reached the cash machine.

"Look Joe, you really shouldn't have paid him."

"Yes, I should. You need to get back. I told you, me and my brother have got this."

Rod shook Joe's hand. "It's been great meeting you. Remember to look me up in the year 2022."

"I most certainly will," replied Joe.

Rod entered the card into the machine. He dialled 1990. Nothing happened.

"Is something wrong?" asked Joe.

"I entered the pin, 1990, but nothing happened."

"Try 2022. See if that will…"

Rod typed in 2022 and Joe stopped mid-sentence. Rod turned around. Joe wasn't there. He was back in 2022. But what he then saw gave him a tremendous shock.

11

The World Turned Upside-Down

Rod gazed in horror at the sight before him. There was rubble everywhere. Not a building in sight. All the shops that had been there were destroyed.

"No!" screamed Rod and kicked the cash machine, the only thing still standing. "This can't be happening! What have I done?"

He gave the cash machine another kick and then he heard the click of a gun.

"Hold it right there, kid, and put your hands in the air."

Rod immediately put his hands up and spun around. A red-haired policewoman was pointing a revolver at him. She quickly walked up to him. "Turn around and put your hands behind your back," she said in her Scottish accent.

Rod did as he was told and felt the cold steel handcuffs being placed on his wrists. He heard them click as they locked.

"Why exactly am I under arrest?" he asked.

"It's under the strict orders of Superbus," the policewoman replied. "Long live the emperor."

"Superbus," said an astonished Rod. "He was a mythical Roman king—the worst one. He was a real tyrant. Surely I haven't gone back in time over two and a half thousand years. What year is it?"

"It's 2022," said the policewoman. "The 2nd of July. It's just a couple of minutes after you left here."

"But I didn't leave this world," said Rod, feeling like his brain was about to explode. "The world I left was normal. All the buildings here were still standing. None of this makes sense."

"I'll explain everything to you, starting from the beginning," said the policewoman as she led Rod to the police car. "There was a man called Agustin De Baerdemaeker."

Rod inwardly groaned as he heard that name. He knew that whatever had happened was his fault. If he hadn't gone back in time, none of this would have happened.

"Agustin was an MP, a backbencher nobody had really heard of," the policewoman continued, as she opened the car door and helped him in. She then got in the car herself, turned on the engine, started driving and continued her story, "In early 2020, a global pandemic, called the Coronavirus, hit. The whole world went into lockdown."

"Yes, I know that," said Rod. "But restrictions were removed just over a year later and life went back to normal."

"You're wrong," said the policewoman surprisingly. "One day in Parliament, Agustin got up and spoke of how little the government had done to stop the virus spreading. He publicly labelled the prime minister a murderer and some of Agustin's supporters actually threw the prime minister out of the Houses of Parliament to his death. Agustin had so many supporters that nobody could stop him becoming prime minister. He then fully locked the country down."

"He actually did that?" asked Rod, his eyes nearly falling out of his head.

"Yes. He ordered the construction of chain fences outside everyone's houses. If anybody left their home without permission, they would be arrested. If any town tried to oppose the construction of the chain fences, it would be destroyed. As you can see, Inglefell was one of those towns.

"When the number of Covid cases dropped, Agustin eased restrictions. After taking on the name Superbus, who he hailed one of the world's best ever leaders in history, his ambitions changed. Superbus was not satisfied with ruling the UK. His aim was world domination."

"Another power-thirsty leader, like Napoleon and Hitler," said Rod to himself, beginning to understand the situation he found himself in.

"Superbus is about to start World War Three. He has ordered that all men and women, regardless of age, join the army. The army training is extremely intense. He is dead keen on victory. He is just about to declare war on France."

"I have a question. If all this is true, why has he ordered the arrest of one ordinary fourteen-year-old boy?"

"You're no ordinary fourteen-year-old, Rodney," said the policewoman, calling by his name for the first time. "You are a time traveller. You met Superbus in 1990. He knows who you are."

"But why does he want me?"

"You really don't remember, do you?" said the policewoman. "Your whole family are prisoners of Superbus. He ordered me to bring you here today, so that you would go back in time."

"You drove me here earlier?"

"I did. I made sure you went back in time, then a couple of minutes later you appeared again."

"But why would he want me to go back in time?"

"Why don't you ask him yourself? You're just about to meet him."

The policewoman parked the car and Rod looked out of the window. A man with grey hair, looking like he was in his late seventies or early eighties approached them.

"How did you get on, Amy?" he asked, looking at the policewoman.

"Quite successfully, Superbus, I think," she replied. "He used the cash machine, disappeared for a couple of minutes and then reappeared. I don't think he remembers anything that has happened in the last couple of years."

"Perfect," said Superbus, stroking his chin. "He must have come straight from when he left that night. Well, Rodney, are you not going to say hello to an old friend?"

"You're certainly old but you're not and never will be my friend," said Rod in a cool tone.

"That's a little ungrateful, don't you think, considering I gave you the card all those years ago and let you return to your future."

"Yeah well, you should have made me stay. You completely spoilt my future. Look at this country. It's mostly rubble. You took a beautiful world and turned it into this. Does this make you feel happy?"

"It does, actually," replied Superbus. "Take him to solitary confinement, Amy. I think Rod needs to spend some time on his own to get used to this."

"You wait till I go back in time, Agustin!" shouted Rod as Amy dragged him away. "I'm going to make sure you don't get away from the police!"

12

Agustin Tells His Story

Rod heard footsteps outside his cell. He lifted up his hands and heard the clink of chains beneath him. Amy had securely fastened his hands and feet into iron manacles, which were chained to the ground, when she locked him in the cell the previous night. She had also removed his card so he couldn't go back to 1990 even if he escaped.

Rod assumed that it was Amy coming with food for him. He looked up and instead saw Superbus standing at the door.

"Come to give me a hiding for being rude to you yesterday?" he sneered.

"If I were you, I'd keep quiet and show some respect. There are many different slow and painful ways I can have you executed."

"You don't scare me," said Rod boldly. Then he paused and looked thoughtful. "Actually, I will give you my respect. But only if you tell me what happened since I left you behind thirty years ago."

"Well, you're not going anywhere anytime soon, so I don't suppose it matters if I tell you my story," said Superbus. "I had lost my job as a policeman. I probably told you this thirty years ago. I was a wanted criminal, and the police had a court case going on against me. With all the money I had made from people's bribes, I had enough money to make the whole case disappear. I was a free man again."

"What happened that night?" asked Rod. "The police were on their way to arrest you. How did you escape?"

"Your so-called plan to catch me happened to be overheard by my son, Tom. Now, he came and told me everything and we also made a plan. We would lure you in, get you sent back to this year and out of our way and make a large sum of money.

"Our plan worked perfectly and as we knew the police were on their way, we took the bus to the nearest town, stayed the night in a hotel and fled up north.

"About a year later, when I had made enough money, I turned myself in. I was charged with several crimes of course, but I had made enough money to have some decent lawyers and I was found not guilty. Of course, I had to spend a few months in prison for hiding from the police, but after that, I was a free man.

"I had already studied law to become a policeman, so I decided to become a Member of Parliament. I was elected in the 1997 General Election. Shortly after being elected, I saw a speech therapist because I knew that if I was to have any chance of having a successful career as an MP, I would have to give a lot of speeches. And I wasn't able to do that when I couldn't speak properly—"

"Oh, that's what happened, was it?" interrupted Rod. "I thought that you'd just managed to earn enough money to buy some h's."

"Hold your tongue!" bellowed Superbus. "And learn some manners too, interrupting my fabulous story like that.

As I was saying, I became an MP in 1997 and faithfully served this country as a backbencher for over twenty years. But I realised that all the Prime Ministers were the same, they didn't care about the country, they only cared about themselves.

"After the Covid pandemic hit, I decided enough was enough. Many people felt the same way, a lot of MPs too. When I had sufficient support, I made my move. I was going to personally remove the prime minister from Parliament and usurp his rule.

"All my supporters were in unanimous agreement. When the timing was right, I acted. Everything went according to plan. I became in charge of this country. And then I realised something. Our previous leaders were too content with ruling just Great Britain.

"This country has so much potential. We had the biggest empire this world has ever seen, just over 100 years ago. The British Empire was the best thing that ever happened to this world. I intend to restore it, starting with the invasion of France.

"Soon the whole of Europe will be mine, then Asia, Africa and the Americas. Then I will rule the whole world. No one can stop me. I am invincible."

"I have a question for you," said Rod, interrupting Superbus' thoughts of world dominion. "Why did you get me to go back in time? Amy said that she took me to that very same cash machine earlier just so I could go back in time. Why was this?"

"You see, Rodney," replied Superbus. "When you get to my age, you become wise. And I consider myself a very wise person after all I have achieved. Now, I remember you telling me all those years ago that you had time-travelled from the year 2022. When I first became leader of this country, it got me thinking.

"You see, I knew that all that had happened in the past thirty years would never have happened had I been arrested that night you set the trap. I then realised that if you did not go back in time, the past thirty years would have been rewritten. All that I have achieved would be for nothing.

"That is the reason I captured your family. I had my eye on you, and I couldn't risk you escaping. I needed you to go back in time. I had to make sure that the past did not change."

"So you're saying that it's my fault?" said Rod quietly. "It really is my fault. If I hadn't gone back in time, you would never have been the leader of this country. Oh, what have I done?"

13

A Family Reunion

Superbus, surprisingly, went up to Rod and unlocked his chains. He helped Rod onto his feet.

"I think there's some people you want to see, Rod," said Superbus in a friendly tone.

They walked out of the cell, into the corridor and after passing a few doors, Superbus unlocked a door and opened it. Rod looked inside and saw his family.

"ROD!" they all cried and ran towards the door. Superbus gave Rod a little shove inside and closed the door. Rod's family immediately mobbed him.

"Oh Rod, it's been days since we last saw you," cried Rosie. "Where have you been?"

"It's a very long story," said Rod. "Let's just say that things have changed a great deal since I last saw you all."

"I think I know where you went, Rod," said Sandy, unexpectedly. "You time-travelled to 1990, didn't you? I remember you; it was when I was seventeen."

"How long have you known, Dad?" Rod asked. "When did you realise that I had lied to you?"

"It was a couple of months after you suddenly disappeared, without saying a word to anyone. When I finally persuaded your grandad to make up with his brother, I went to Bristol to see you again and ask why you had left without saying goodbye. The first person I met was your uncle Robert and he knew nothing of you. No one in the family resembled you in any way.

"Sometime later, I had a chat with your mum about you, and she also said that you looked familiar in a strange way, and even reminded her of herself.

"I was puzzled, I couldn't understand why you would have lied about who you were and how you knew so much about my family. Then I remembered how you called me Dad that time and it clicked; you were my son from the future.

"As you've grown up, it's become more and more clear that you were the Rodney I met all those years ago. And the other day, when they came and took you away, I sort of guessed that you would be going back in time."

"Dad," said Rod, with tears in his eyes, "I am so sorry for lying to you. I just couldn't… I didn't know how to tell you. You wouldn't have believed me."

"Don't worry, Rod," said Sandy reassuringly. "I completely understand. You had to lie given the circumstances. It's not your fault."

"Yes, it is my fault. You don't understand; everything, the situation we're in, it is completely my fault. I changed history when I went back in time."

"What are you talking about, Rod?" asked Sandy, surprised. "This isn't your fault. We were in this situation before you left, remember? Superbus has been in charge for at least two years now. Your time-travel was a result of whatever that horrid man did to you. You did not change the course of history."

"I did," said Rod, looking around. "All of this; this is new to me. Things weren't like this when I time-travelled. Life was normal. The Covid-19 pandemic happened, but Superbus didn't take over and restrictions eased. None of this is supposed to have happened."

A thought came into Rod's mind, and he put his hand in his pocket; he pulled out the newspaper article he had in there. It was no longer blank. The article was headlined, *Criminal Cop Case Concerns Chief Constables*.

Rod read how the police were looking for Agustin all over the country but were unable to find him. There had been reports of him being sighted in Inglefell, but when the police came to investigate, he was long gone. The police feared he had escaped the country.

"Read this," said Rod, as he passed the newspaper article around. "I tore it out of an old newspaper in the attic at home a few days ago. It was in the old cardboard box along with this t-shirt I'm wearing. This is your old England t-shirt, Dad. Hope you don't mind me wearing it.

"The reason I tore the article out of the newspaper was because it mentioned our village, Inglefell. It said he was captured in Inglefell, our very own village. The article said that Superbus was arrested and sentenced to fifteen years in prison.

"I went back in time, and because of it, he escaped from the police. This is all my fault. Things were amazing when I left; we were about to celebrate your thirtieth anniversary."

"Good gracious," said Louise in astonishment. "It's our thirtieth anniversary today and we had completely forgotten about—"

BANG! BANG! BANG! There was a thunderous knock at the cell door. The key turned in the lock and the door swung open.

"Guys, get your stuff ready!" yelled a guy in camouflage. He was obviously an army commander. Rod immediately recognised him. He was the guy who worked in the local corner shop, at least he did in his world. Now, what was his name, Tony, Timothy, Thomas… Tom! It was Tom, how could he have forgotten his name!

"Come on, hurry up!" he shouted. "We're leaving for France in ten minutes."

The MacDoodle family hurriedly packed their bags, which were in their cell.

"Why are we going to France?" whispered Rod.

"Do you really not know?" said Louise. "We've known about this for weeks. Superbus is invading France. He expects everyone, who is able, to fight for their country."

14

Return of an Old Friend

There were many army trucks, being loaded with people in the car park outside. Rod noticed a frail old man and was appalled to see that he was also having to fight for his country. *He must be nearly seventy,* Rod thought.

The man seemed to be aware that Rod was looking at him, and he looked up, straight at Rod. As their eyes met, they instantly recognised each other.

"Joe!" cried Rod and ran up to hug him. "It's so good to see you again. It's only been a few days since I last saw you, but it must be many years since you last saw me."

"Yes, many years indeed," replied Joe, forcing a smile. "I'm not going to lie; life has been quite tough for me since we met."

"Oh no," said Rod quietly. "I am so sorry, Joe. What happened?"

"Trust me, Rod, you do not want to know," replied Joe.

"Look," said Rod, "I need to escape and get back to the night I left. The way things are now, this isn't what life was like for me growing up. I need to go back and put things right. Any information you can give me about the events after that night could be crucial."

Joe sighed, knowing Rod was right and began to tell his story.

"Just after you left, Agustin and Tom found me again. They were really mad and there were two of them. There wasn't much I could do to defend myself. I remember being woken up a couple of hours later by my brother. Several policemen had arrived but there was no trace of Agustin; he had fled the district.

"We searched high and low for Agustin over the next few months. There were several reports of sightings, but there was no sign of him whenever we followed these reports. My brother was convinced that he had gone abroad, so he contacted the authorities in several European countries, but nothing came of it.

"Then one day, Agustin came and turned himself in. We were stunned. It came out of nowhere. We immediately started a court case in the Crown Court. We had several criminal charges against him. We were certain he would get at least fifteen years behind bars."

At this point, the newspaper article flashed into Rod's mind. He remembered reading it a few days before. Agustin had been convicted and sentenced to fifteen years behind bars. With a sinking feeling, Rod knew he had messed this up.

"The court case was rigged, I'm sure of it," Joe said in an angry tone. "The jury found him not guilty of all charges. None of us could believe it. Of course, Agustin spent a few months behind bars due to running and hiding from the police, but there was nothing we could do to prevent his release.

"That's when the trouble really started for me. My brother's superior felt he had made a complete mess of the situation, and he got the sack. My brother blamed me; he felt

I could have done more to prevent Agustin from escaping Inglefell.

"He completely stopped working and coerced me into giving him half of my wages. I felt so guilty about the whole affair that I quickly agreed to this. I had to work twice as much in order to make the same income. I burnt myself out working these long hours, well over fifteen hours a day. I would go to bed straight after coming home from work. I couldn't sleep much, so I would wake up tired and then my quality of work wouldn't be very good. I eventually had to give up work, causing the family to fall upon hard times.

"We had also been trying to keep an eye on Agustin during this time. He went under the radar for the first few years, but then he decided to stand for MP in a nearby constituency.

"Both me and my brother tried speaking to constituents, persuading them not to vote for him, but they wouldn't listen. My brother was disgraced after losing his job as superintendent; they wouldn't listen to anything he said. Agustin served as a backbencher for many years. But then came the Covid pandemic and then—"

"I know," interrupted Rod quietly, feeling incredibly guilty about the situation. "I've heard all about it. I am so sorry to have caused you all this trouble. Hearing this has made me all the more determined to go back and put it right. And now, I know exactly what we need to do; we need to escape right now."

"How can we escape though?" asked Joe. "They're taking us to France now. It's so crowded, we'll never be able to escape here."

Rod looked around. There were so many people, it would be almost impossible to escape. Then he noticed one of the army trucks. It was empty and the key was in the ignition. If only they could get there quickly without being seen.

Then Rod remembered that Amy had taken his card the previous night. He saw her walking in their direction and an idea flashed into his mind. She was wearing the same clothes that she had worn the previous day. He knew that Amy had put the card in her pocket. What if it was still there? He needed a distraction for his plan.

"Distract Amy," he whispered to Joe. "Talk to her about something. She may have my card in her pocket, which we need to go back in time. I'm going to try and pickpocket her."

"Okay, but be careful," said Joe. "Hey Amy, can I talk to you about something?"

"What is it?" she replied. "As you can see, I'm very busy."

"Look," said Joe. "I'm sixty-five. Surely I'm too old to be going off to war in France? How is it right to send an old man into battle like this?"

"Joe, we've been through this before," said Amy. "Superbus has ordered that everyone who is able to fight must go to France and fight for the country. You have to do this— you aren't exempt from military service."

Joe glanced at Rod and saw that he had the card in his hand. The distraction had worked.

"It still isn't right," he said to Amy.

"Look, there are many things I need to do at the moment. Stop wasting my time," said Amy as she walked off.

"Got it," said Rod, smiling as he showed Joe the card. "See that truck there? Well, the keys are in the ignition. If we make our way there quickly, we can escape."

"Just walk there slowly," said Joe quietly. "We don't want to make a scene. When we reach the car, get in the passenger's seat. I'll drive."

"No, Joe," replied Rod. "You're not well enough to drive. I will drive the truck."

"But you're fourteen. You're not allowed to drive."

"Just because I'm not allowed, it doesn't mean I don't know how to drive. Now we're wasting time by arguing. Quickly, get in the passenger's seat."

Joe reluctantly climbed into the passenger's side as Rod went behind the wheel.

"Are you sure you know what you're doing?" he asked Rod.

Rod nodded and turned the key. The engine roared into life. Rod put the truck into gear, and they started moving. The truck sped up and he swerved dangerously around everyone, trying not to knock anyone over.

"Watch out, Dad!" yelled Tom as the truck nearly crashed into Superbus.

Superbus jumped out of the way in time and spun around. He cried in horror when he saw who was driving.

"We've got to stop them!" he shouted at Tom and Amy. "If they go back to 1990, they could ruin everything."

"It's okay," said Amy. "I took Rod's card last night so he can't get back. I put it right here in this pocket."

Amy put her hands in her pockets, trying to find the card.

"Oh no, it's not here. Rod must have taken it when I wasn't looking."

"Right, you two, in this truck now," ordered Agustin. "We've got to catch them before they get away."

15

The Great Escape

Rod had been driving at top speed for quite a while. He knew the way to Inglefell. It wasn't too far away now. However, there wasn't much fuel left in the tank of the truck. He wasn't sure whether the truck would make it all the way.

He cast his thoughts back to when he had nearly run Superbus over. What had Tom yelled? Didn't he say, "Watch out, Dad!"? It suddenly dawned on him; this was Superbus' son, the boy who had beaten him and Sandy up that night. The guy he had known all his life, working behind the counter at the local corner shop, was him.

Rod was completely astonished. He had always known Tom to be very friendly when serving behind the counter. And yet he was a mean, horrible bully when he was younger. Rod couldn't believe they were the same person.

Joe, who was sitting next to Rod, turned around and saw Superbus behind.

"Quick, Rod," he urged. "They're right behind us. We have to speed up or they'll catch us."

"This is the fastest the truck will go," said Rod. "The fuel tank is almost empty too. We're going to have to pull over and leg it to the cash machine."

"We can't run all that way, Rod," said Joe. "Inglefell is over a mile away. We'll never make it."

"We have to," said Rod. "It's our only chance."

"No," said Joe. "Not we, you. There's no way I can run that far. You will need to do this on your own. Don't worry about me, I can hold them up. Jump out and I'll take over the driving."

Rod slowed the car down and hopped out. He landed on his feet and was away at top speed. Joe slid across so he was behind the wheel. He spun the truck around and blocked the road. There was no way that Superbus could get around it.

Joe quickly climbed out and took cover behind a large rock. Superbus saw the truck blocking the road and gave a loud roar. He tried to go around the truck, but the ground each side of the truck was muddy and waterlogged. The engine spluttered and gave out.

"You stupid, foolish man!" yelled Superbus, spotting Joe hiding behind the rock. "You've ruined everything."

"Look, Dad," said Tom, pointing in the distance. "There's Rod."

"Well, don't just stand there," said Superbus frustratedly. "Run after him. Don't let him reach that cash machine."

Tom jumped out of the truck into the mud below. He tried to move his feet, but they wouldn't budge.

"Hurry up, what's taking you so long?" shouted Superbus.

"My feet, they're stuck," said Tom in annoyance. "They won't move."

"Come on, son," yelled Superbus. "Pull harder. What are you? A man or a mouse?"

Tom, feeling humiliated by his dad's insults, used all his strength and gave one huge shove. His feet came free quickly, but Tom lost his balance and faceplanted into the mud. He stood up, covered from head to toe in filthy, brown mud. Amy couldn't stop herself from laughing.

"Don't stand there laughing at me!" yelled Tom. "Get out and run after him."

Instead of climbing out of the side into the mud, Amy slid gracefully down the bonnet and landed on dry ground. She immediately took to her heels and tore after Rod, who by now was out of sight.

Rod was running as fast as he could. His lungs were bursting. His breathing was heavy. He wasn't used to running this fast for so long.

Rod knew that he would have to stop for breath soon. As he went around the corner, he caught sight of Inglefell and breathed a huge sigh of relief. he was there. He could see the cash machine in the distance, a couple of hundred yards away.

Rod suddenly heard a yell from behind him. He quickly looked around and his heart sank. Amy was about fifty yards behind him—she had almost caught up.

"Stop!" yelled Amy, as Rod sprinted towards the cash machine, which was now less than a hundred yards away.

Rod didn't listen. He slid his hand into his pocket and pulled out the card. He was now within touching distance of the machine.

Rod slowed to avoid crashing into the machine. He reached out his hand to insert the card into the machine. He was about to do it. He was about to escape.

Amy was right behind Rod now. She saw him about to insert the card and knew she had to act. Amy dived for Rod's ankles.

Bang. Rod's skull crashed against the cash machine and the card went flying.

"No!" bellowed Rod in anger and disappointment. He immediately tried to get up on his feet. However, Amy was too quick for him. She was on him in an instant. Rod was pinned to the ground.

"Give up," said Amy menacingly. "You can't win."

"Let me go," pleaded Rod, as he tried to struggle and throw Amy off him. "This isn't right, none of what is happening at the moment is right, and you know it. There's war and destruction. People suffering all around. You have to let me go back and change this."

"No," said Amy. "Superbus has been like a father to me. He is responsible for my position as second-in-command to him. I can't betray him like this."

"Amy," said Rod. "You don't like him; you know how evil he is, that what he's doing is wrong. You don't owe him anything. Yes, he has looked after and cared for you. But look at what he's doing.

"Look at this village. He destroyed it. All these buildings in ruins. This used to be somewhere people lived happily, got on well with each other, enjoyed life. Superbus destroyed all this, and he will continue to do so in every other country if you don't let me go back and stop—"

Parp, Parp! A car horn interrupted Rod. Amy turned around and saw Superbus driving towards them in an army truck. He had managed to wrestle the key off Joe and drive the truck all the way there.

The fuel had lasted all the way there. But not for long. The truck coughed and spluttered and came to a stop. Agustin tried to restart the engine. Nothing happened. The truck was dead.

Agustin hopped out and ran over towards Amy and Rod, who were about a hundred yards away.

While Amy watched him run towards them, she briefly relieved the pressure in her left arm, which was pinning Rod's right arm to the ground. Rod felt the release of pressure. Now was his chance.

"Superbus, how did you…" began Amy, before realising she had lifted her arm. Cursing herself, she quickly turned to grab Rod's arm again, having felt him pull it away. But it was too late.

Crash. Rod's fist went straight into Amy's face. As she fell back, Rod managed to wriggle himself free. He immediately pushed himself up onto his feet and picked up the card off the floor.

"Get after him, Amy!" yelled Superbus, seeing Rod inserting the card into the cash machine. "Don't let him get away!"

Amy rose to her feet quickly. She made a despairing dive for Rod's feet again. Rod entered the pin into the machine. Amy reached out and tried to grab his legs. She brought her hands together.

Smack. Amy's hands hit together. Rod's legs were no longer there. In fact, Rod was no longer there. He had gone. He was back in 1990.

16

The Hunt for Agustin Begins

Rod turned around from the cash machine and, to his immense relief, he saw buildings. Everything in Inglefell was how it should be. Except, of course, he was thirty-two years in the past. Now, he had to put things right.

Rod had decided the first thing he needed to do was to find Joe. Obviously, he needed to check that Joe was alright after the previous night's events. Rod also needed Joe's help if he was to stop Superbus from escaping. Agustin actually, as he hadn't changed his name yet.

Rod looked at the cash machine and noticed the date. It was 7 July 1990. He had come back a day after he had left. Agustin must have already left. This made it all the more harder to find him, but he had to.

Rod saw a police car outside a house nearby. He quickly made his way over. He needed to get the police to make a search for Agustin, before it was too late. Before Agustin would have the money to fix the court case and get away free.

The police car was empty. Rod turned around and looked at the house the car was outside. The front door suddenly opened and who should walk out but Joe, helped by a couple of policemen.

"Joe!" yelled Rod, running up to him. As he approached Joe, he noticed all the bruises on his face. He remembered what Joe had said about the night he had left. Those bruises must have been caused by Agustin.

"Rod," said Joe in surprise, "how are you here? I saw you go back to your future myself."

"I know," said Rod, grinning. "But now I'm back and I'm here to stay until we have caught Agustin."

"But why?" asked Joe. "Why would you come back to help us look for him?"

"You see these buildings?" said Rod. "None of them were standing when I went back. This whole village was a pile of rubble. It was all Agustin's doing. He was in charge of the country, and he was about to start World War Three."

"Right," said Joe. "Well, obviously, we need you to help us find him, because if we searched on our own, we would be unsuccessful, as you managed to find out."

"Basically, it took you guys over a year to find him," informed Rod. "He actually turned himself in, knowing he had made enough money to fix the court case and be acquitted of all the charges you planned to bring against him. So, the sooner we find him, the better."

"You seem to know a lot about what has happened in the years since now," said Joe. "Do you know anything about what Agustin did shortly after the night you left?"

"That I do," replied Rod, grinning. "He told me himself. He said he took the bus, with his son to a nearby town, and stayed the night in a hotel. He said that he fled the district, the next day and went north."

The two policemen, who were standing next to Joe, began to talk amongst themselves quietly. One of them then decided to speak to Rod.

"Are you sure they definitely took the bus last night?" he asked.

"Yes," said Rod. "It was fairly soon after I left."

"Great," the policeman replied. "My colleague just told me that on a Friday night after eight o'clock, the buses only run from here to Braunwald. Joe said it was about half eight when you went back so Agustin must have gone to Braunwald. And you say he stayed the night in a hotel?"

Seeing Rod nod his head, the policeman again spoke quietly to his colleague. He seemed quite pleased with what his colleague told him.

"Apparently, there's only one hotel in Braunwald, so that should make it easier to find him."

"What are we waiting for?" Rod asked excitedly. "Let's go there now and find him."

"Now, hold on a moment," the policeman replied. "Look at my brother's face. This is what Agustin did to him last night. He is a dangerous criminal, so we need to plan things carefully before we go rushing in.

"Now, it's currently midday. As Agustin is a wanted criminal, he is likely to have already left Braunwald by now. However, there is a chance he is still there.

"Therefore, we will block off all the road exits in Braunwald and search the hotel and town centre. We will also send a search party north of Braunwald, to search through several of the villages he may have stopped in. Did he give you any indication of where he went after Braunwald?"

"No sir," replied Rod. "But I have a feeling it was quite a long way north."

"Right, thank you," the policeman said, before barking a few orders into his walkie-talkie. "We're heading off now to Braunwald. Whatever you do, don't leave here. I do not want you to be anywhere near Agustin. You've done a fantastic job already in giving us all this information. Leave it to us to do the rest."

17

A Kidnap and an Arrest

Rod jogged alongside the road to Braunwald, having completely disregarded the policeman's orders; well, the superintendent's actually. Rod had just worked this out as he had called Joe his brother and Joe had told him that his brother was the superintendent of the district.

Rod just wanted to be part of the action somehow. He felt responsible for Agustin's escape and wanted to make up for it by finding him. Rod had intended to take the bus from Inglefell to Braunwald. However, on Saturdays, only a couple of buses travelled through Braunwald, and they didn't run until late afternoon.

Once Rod had reached Braunwald, he silently made his way through the town, taking care not to be spotted by any policemen. Without realising it, Rod had taken a path that led out of the town centre. He soon came to a quiet country road and realised he had taken a wrong turn.

Rod was about to go back when he suddenly heard a car engine. He walked round the corner and spotted the car. He quietly made his way to it. It was empty.

He began to feel suspicious. Why would somebody just leave their car here with its engine running? Something fishy was going on and Rod sensed Agustin just might be behind it.

Rod turned around and there was Agustin standing right in front of him.

"Well, if it ain't young Rodney 'ere," said Agustin in a menacing tone. "Can't keep yourself outta no trouble I see. You know you almost 'ad me fooled when you disappeared last night. I 'alf fought you'd gone back to your future. But I sorta guessed you might be back and 'ere you are."

Rod suddenly found himself being seized from behind. He tried to let out a yell, but a hand came over his mouth.

"Yer know, I was being very generous to yer last night by lettin' yer go back. Well, this time yer ain't gonna be so lucky. I'm afraid you're comin' wiv me."

Rod felt a needle being poked into his neck. Something was being injected into his body. Everything in front of him started spinning and then went black.

Rod painfully opened his eyes. He saw a car roof over his head. He was lying on the back seats of a car. He tried to move his hands to rub his eyes but found they had been tightly bound behind his back. His mouth had also been gagged so he couldn't shout.

Rod tried to sit up but fell back down quickly. Agustin spotted the movement in the rear-view mirror.

"I fought you gave 'im enough dose to knock 'im out for six hours," he said savagely to Tom.

"I did, Dad," Tom replied. "But I must have spilled some accidentally."

"You foolish boy," muttered Agustin. "If 'e 'ad woken up at an inconvenient time, it could 'ave ruined everything."

"I'm sorry, Dad," said Tom quietly.

"You're sorry?" barked Agustin. "Sorry ain't good enough. This ain't the first time you've done something like this. Yer don't 'alf disappoint me son."

The car slowed to a halt. Agustin turned and looked at Tom. "Get outta the car," he said.

"What do you mean?" Tom asked. "Dad, what's going on?"

"Just get out."

Tom got out and closed the door. Agustin quickly accelerated and moved off. Tom tried to grab the door handle, but he couldn't hold on. He had been left at the side of the road.

Rod had watched the whole scene with astonishment. He felt very sorry for Tom, being treated the way he just was. It almost made him feel like forgiving him for beating up him and Sandy that night. Almost.

Rod's eyes started to feel heavy. The effects of the drug he had been given had not yet worn off. His eyes gradually began to close. And he was fast asleep.

The back door of the car opened, and Rod awoke with a start. The front seat was empty, Agustin had disappeared again. Rod saw a policeman at the door and relief flooded into him. He had been found. He was safe.

"I thought I told you to stay put," said the policeman in an icy tone, as he untied Rod.

Rod recognised the voice. It was Joe's brother, the superintendent.

"I'm really sorry, sir, I should have listened to you."

"You most certainly should have. You were in very serious danger. You could have been killed. Luckily, the driver of a police car noticed that the car you were in was a stolen one. The driver of your car tried to outrun the police, but I think that the car broke down. He got out of the car and fled. But we were ready for it, we had him covered. He didn't make it far before he was captured."

Rod looked round and saw Agustin, in handcuffs, being shoved into a police van. He could not believe what had just happened. He then saw Tom, Agustin's son, walk up to him.

"So, Rod," he said cheerfully, "aren't you going to thank the guy who saved your life?"

18

How Tom Became a Hero

A Few Hours Earlier

The car engine coughed and spluttered. Agustin gave a frustrated groan as he kept trying to turn the key in the ignition.

"No, why won't you start?" he yelled. "We need to get away quickly."

Agustin and Tom had spent the night in a hotel in Braunwald and were hoping to have an early start. Unfortunately for them, the buses weren't running that morning, and they would have to wait until late afternoon for the first one.

They decided to walk quickly out of Braunwald and make their way to a nearby town, from where they could catch a bus. However, to their delight, they had come across an abandoned car as they walked. The keys were also in the ignition. But their joy soon turned to frustration when they realised they couldn't get the car to start.

"It's okay, Dad," Tom said reassuringly. "My friend is a mechanic. He will come and fix it for us."

"You need to be careful," warned Agustin. "This ain't our car, it may even be stolen. I am also a wanted criminal. If your friend finds this out, we're in big trouble."

"Don't worry," said Tom. "I trust him. He won't snoop or ask questions."

"Well, just to be safe, I'll go and 'ide in our 'spot'. Come and get me once the car is fixed and then we can get on our way."

Tom called out his friend, who had a look at the car. He found that it had a flat battery.

"I can jumpstart the car, but really you need to get the battery replaced. I don't have any spares on me at the moment, so I can't do that now."

"Don't worry," said Tom. "How long will this car run for before the battery goes again?"

"Sixty miles max," Tom's friend replied. "Wherever you're going tonight, make sure that you replace the battery there."

Once the engine had been jumpstarted and roared into life, Tom went to fetch Agustin. He didn't dare switch off the engine in case the battery died again. As Tom and Agustin came back, they saw someone by the car, looking in at the window.

"Quick, get back," hissed Agustin. Then he looked more closely at the figure and recognised him. "Actually, don't worry. It's Rod. Snooping around again where 'e's not wanted. This time we'll teach 'im a lesson."

Agustin reached into his pocket and pulled out a syringe. He quickly poured some liquid into it and gave it to Tom.

"'ere, grab 'old of Rod and inject this into 'im. I'll distract 'im so 'e don't notice you come up on 'im. There's enough dose in 'ere to knock 'im out for six hours."

Tom quietly made his way round the car without being spotted. He then saw his dad approach Rod. Now was his chance. He quickly went up to Rod and grabbed him. However, his arm twitched and some of the drug came out. He moaned to himself quietly before injecting the rest of the dose into Rod. Rod's body went limp and Tom lowered him to the ground gently.

Agustin pulled a knife out of his pocket. He walked over to a tree where a rope swing was hanging from a branch. Agustin held the rope at his highest reach and began to cut down the swing with his knife.

Once the swing had fallen from the tree, Agustin loosed the small seat branch and threw the rope over to Tom.

"'ere, tie 'im up wiv this. There's an 'andkerchief 'ere in me pocket which you can use to gag 'im."

Tom quickly bound Rod with the rope. Agustin opened the back door of the car and walked over to Rod. Together, he and Tom picked up Rod and slid him onto the back seat. Then they both hopped in the front seats and drove off.

As the car drove along the roads, Tom looked out of the window feeling sick with worry. He knew he hadn't given Rod enough of the dose to knock him out for very long. Soon Rod would be awake, and his dad would not be pleased.

Tom caught sight of Rod stirring and his heart sank. He desperately hoped Agustin hadn't noticed, but he had. And then the big argument came, which resulted in Agustin ordering him to get out of the car.

Tom was absolutely furious when Agustin drove off. How dare he treat him this way? How dare he be so angry at such a small mistake?

This was the last straw for Tom. Too many times had he been treated like this. Not anymore. Tom knew what he had to do. He had to call the police and turn Agustin in.

Deep down, Tom had always known this was what he should have done. But Agustin was his dad, and he just hadn't been able to betray him—until now. Agustin had deserted him at the side of the road. This caused Tom to see red and act fast.

Tom ran to the nearest village. He found the police station and burst in. After Tom stammered out everything to a surprised policeman, the police were on their way. Tom knew exactly where Agustin and Rod were headed as they had made plans earlier.

Agustin, however, had suspected that Tom may betray him so had changed plans and headed in a totally different direction. What Agustin did not know was that the car's battery was about to die, as Tom hadn't told him the car would only go for another sixty miles or so.

Agustin cried in horror as he heard the sound of a siren behind. He looked in his rear-view mirror, and there it was— a police car on his tail. He desperately tried to speed up the car and break away, but after hearing the sound of the engine about to give out, decided to pull over and make a run for it.

The police saw him emerge from the car and sprint away. They were after him in a flash and managed to round him up without much difficulty. Soon Agustin was in handcuffs and being shoved into the back of a police van.

The court case was brisk; Agustin didn't have much of a defence and was convicted of all charges. He was sentenced to a minimum of fifteen years in prison. Rod's plan to thwart Agustin had succeeded and he was hopeful of returning to a bright future, just as it was when he had left all those days ago.

19

The Anniversary Dinner

Rod once again walked up to the cash machine, about to do yet another time-travel. This time, he hoped it would be his last ever one—the return to 2022, just as he had left it first time.

He was accompanied by Joe, Tom and the superintendent. They all wanted to bid him farewell for the last time.

"Thanks, Joe, for all your help," said Rod, shaking his hand. "I really couldn't have done this without you."

"It was my pleasure," replied Joe with a smile. "And thank you for helping us arrest one of the most dangerous criminals around. My brother and I are extremely grateful for your support."

"That's right, Rod," said the superintendent. "You did a fine job. Take care of and try and keep yourself out of trouble."

"Oh, I will," replied Rod grinning, before turning to Tom. "I can't thank you enough for saving my life. If you hadn't gone to the police, I don't—"

"It's fine," interrupted Tom. "It was the least I could do after being so nasty to you. From now on, I'll try to be much nicer to people."

"I'm sure you will," said Rod reassuringly. "I know you from my future, and I must say, you are a very generous person."

Rod saw Tom blushing and decided he should probably leave before he gave anything else away about the future. He pulled his card out of his pocket and entered it into the machine. He turned around and waved goodbye for a last time, before entering the pin.

The next time Rod turned around, everything was back to normal for him. The shops were still standing this time and they looked exactly as they had when he had left. The cars in the carpark were modern too. He even noticed that brand-new Tesla again.

As Rod took the card out of the machine, he looked at the date on the screen; it was 2 July 2022. This was the same day he had left. It was exactly the same time as well. Not one minute had passed since he had first entered the card into the machine.

Rod sprinted home. He just had to get back and see everyone again: Mum, Dad, Rosie, Dennis. As he ran, he almost knocked over two guys walking along the pavement.

"Hey, watch it," one of them yelled.

"Sorry," Rod cried as he carried on running. He was almost home now. He had just run onto his road. He tore round the corner and there it was; a very welcome sight for Rod.

Rod burst through the front door and went straight into the kitchen where his mum was cooking the dinner.

"Mum," he cried as he saw her, giving her a big hug.

"Rod," she said in amazement, "what on earth is the matter?"

"I'm just glad to be back," replied Rod contentedly.

"But you left just a few minutes ago," said Louise, feeling very puzzled by Rod's behaviour. "Didn't you get any potatoes?"

"Potatoes?" asked Rod, wondering what his mum was talking about. Then it came back to him. His mum had asked him to buy some potatoes which was why he had gone down to the store in the first place.

"You forgot to get them? Oh Rod, you really are…"

"No, mum. It's a cash-only weekend at the store as the card-readers there have broken. The cash machine outside was malfunctioning, so I couldn't get any cash."

"Oh," said Louise, feeling relieved that Rod hadn't gone completely mad, though she still couldn't understand why Rod had been acting so weird. "Well, here's some cash. Come back with the potatoes this time."

"Will do," replied Rod as he walked out again.

Lousie shook her head as she went back to get on with the dinner. Sometimes she did wonder what went through that boy's head.

Rod walked back to the store again, passing the two guys he had almost knocked over when he ran home.

"About what happened earlier," one of them called out.

"Another time," replied Rod, trying not to let himself get distracted again from buying these potatoes.

Rod saw Tom serving behind one of the tills as he entered the store. Once he had picked up the potatoes, Rod made his way to Tom's till.

"I've just got back from 1990," he whispered as Tom scanned the bag of potatoes.

"You did?" replied Tom, his face lighting up. "I've always wondered when you would time-travel, each time I've served you. I'm surprised you recognised me."

"Not really," said Rod, handing over the money. "I actually went to a future, this year in fact, and it was quite different. Both you and Agustin were there, and you called Agustin, 'Dad'. This made me realise that you and Agustin's Tom were one and the same."

"Wow, that must have been a very different future. My dad died in prison over twenty years ago."

"It certainly was," said Rod, turning to leave. "I had to go back to 1990 again to help the police arrest him."

"Oh, so that's what happened," said Tom. "I was very confused when I saw you turn up the day after you had first disappeared through the cash machine."

As Rod turned around to walk out of the store, he spotted the two guys for a third time that morning.

"Paying by cash, not card?" one of them asked.

"How is this any of your business?" Rod asked. He was now starting to freak out. Who were these men and why were they so interested in his payment method?

Rod took to his heels and sprinted home again, anxious to throw these guys off his tail.

The guests soon began to arrive. Most of the people were his parents' work colleagues so Rod didn't recognise them. A few family friends had arrived, so Rod chatted to some of them as they all waited for the dinner to be served.

"Hallo Rod," someone called out.

Rod turned around. It was Joe, only he wasn't looking quite so old as he had in the future Rod had previously returned to. Most of his hair was still dark and his face looked a lot younger.

"Joe," he said in surprise, "what are you doing here?"

"Your dad invited me; we work together at the same company."

Rod couldn't believe this. Joe and his dad worked together. This was unreal. As he cast his eyes around to the front door, he spotted a red-haired woman entering. It was Amy. Her too? Not another work colleague, surely?

Rod made his way over to Amy, who was talking to his mum. Louise caught sight of Rod approaching.

"Rod," she said, "have you met my friend, Amy Williams? She's one of my closest friends at work."

Amy gazed at Rod closely. He looked familiar to her, as if she had once seen him in a dream, but she couldn't quite place him. She turned to Louise and shook her head. "No, I don't think we've met before, at least not that I can remember."

"I didn't think you'd met," said Louise, looking at her watch. "You must excuse me, Amy, I really need to get the shepherd's pie out of the oven."

As Louise walked into the kitchen, Amy turned and spoke to Rod, "You do look strangely familiar. Are you sure we haven't met?"

"Umm, well, I'm not sure," stuttered Rod. He didn't know what to say, he didn't want to lie, but he wasn't quite sure how to tell the truth. Rod caught sight of movement outside the front door and looked up. It was those two guys again.

"Why do they keep following me about?" he murmured aloud.

"Why do who..." asked Amy before stopping and frowning as she caught sight of them. "Excuse me for a moment."

Rod saw Amy walk over to them and say something, though he couldn't quite hear what she said. After a moment, they turned and walked away. Rod hoped that that was the last he would see of them.

"I hope they don't come back," Rod said to Amy as she returned.

"They won't," Amy replied. "I just told them to—"

"Everyone!" yelled Sandy from the kitchen. "Gather around the table, dinner is about to be served."

After a delicious dinner of shepherd's pie, Sandy got up to deliver a speech about his thirty years of marriage.

"As you all know, today is the thirtieth anniversary of my marriage to my beautiful wife, Louise. I simply cannot believe that our wedding was thirty years ago.

"It only seems like yesterday when I was out walking that night with a friend. A group of lads came out of nowhere and beat us both up. We were both lying unconscious on the ground when who should come jogging past but Louise."

Rod went red as he heard this. He knew the friend his dad was talking about was himself. He noticed that his dad was looking at him, and he turned and looked into Sandy's eyes. They both smiled at each other and nodded. Sandy knew that it was his son, Rod, who had been with him that night.

Rod then turned to Louise, who was also looking at him with a smile. She knew as well. A smile spread across Rod's face from ear to ear. Life was back to normal. Both his parents knew about his time-travel and weren't cross with him. Rod sat back and hoped that this moment would never end.

www.ingramcontent.com/pod-product-compliance
Lightning Source LLC
Chambersburg PA
CBHW071454030726
47593CB00003B/993